The All
Crime Detectives

The All Bengali Crime Detectives

Suparna Chatterjee

RUPA
PUBLICATIONS INDIA

First Published 2011
Second Impression 2011

Published by
Rupa Publications India Pvt. Ltd.
7/16, Ansari Road, Daryaganj,
New Delhi 110 002
Sales Centres:

Allahabad Bengaluru Chennai
Hyderabad Jaipur Kathmandu
Kolkata Mumbai

Typeset in Adobe Garamond by
Mindways Design
1410 Chiranjiv Tower
43 Nehru Place
New Delhi 110 019

Printed in India by
B.B. Press.
A-37, Sector 67
Noida 201 301

For my parents
and
for Saimama

Contents

Acknowledgements

This being my first book, the list of people I am indebted to is long:

First, my parents, for giving me the best life they possibly could.

My father and his buddies at the bridge club, whose humorous and philosophical takes on life have been the major source of inspiration for this book.

Saimama, who unfortunately did not live to see this in print, but who would have been insanely happy to be holding this in his hands. I am immensely grateful for the long hours we spent in constructive *adda* – on Van Gogh and Chaurasia, Chekov and Truffaut – much to the distress of the non-insomniacs in the household. Throughout my growing years, he has been my friend, philosopher and guide, directing me to all that is worth knowing in life – music, art, humour and meditation.

Khurshed Batliwala, for giving me the confidence I needed to take up writing seriously. A chance e-mail from half-way across the globe – and three years later, he is the friend I don't think twice about imposing on any time of the day.

My teachers who taught us English at school, Ms Sahana Basak and Ms Rita Dasgupta, for making me fall in love with the language.

Enid Blyton, Agatha Christie and Satyajit Ray – three writers who had planted in me a burning desire to become a sleuth. I followed their path and did the next best thing.

The editors at Rupa, especially Debika Roy Choudhry, for their thoroughness and friendly support.

And last but not the very least, Kanchan, my harshest critic and fiercest supporter, who would effortlessly switch from his academic world of 'bounded rationality' and 'stochastic dominance' to the fictional world of my characters, pointing out in seconds, flaws in the plot I had spent weeks developing. I can never thank God enough for bringing him into my life!

A New Routine

Akhil Banerjee lay awake in his bed, contemplating the day that lay ahead of him. He had been awake for quite a while. A sideward glance at the bedside alarm clock told him it was still too early for the rest of the household to be up. Subhadra, his wife of thirty-two years slept contentedly by his side. He had no wish to wake her up. Indeed, he had no wish to be up so early himself. But one couldn't fight with habit, he supposed.

He got off the bed noiselessly, taking care not to disturb Subhadra, and headed for the bathroom down the corridor. One look at his reflection in the plastic-framed mirror above the sink, confirmed his worst fears. He had been waiting for this day for as long as he could remember, often praying that it should arrive much sooner than the law of the land had intended. Yet, today, when that day had finally arrived, he was not sure what to do with it. For the inescapable fact remained, that Akhil Banerjee, Calcutta High Court Judge till a few hours ago, felt he was too young to retire.

Over the next few minutes, during which he brushed his teeth and combed his thinning salt-and-pepper hair that curled up below the ears, he brooded over the enormity of the situation. He was now unemployed, had no fixed routine, had nowhere to rush to, no cases to preside over, no more worthless criminals to sentence. In other words, he had done his duty to society and whether he was ready or not, society had pronounced its sentence. High Court Judge Akhil Banerjee would now lead a life of retirement. Retirement, he winced at the word.

He climbed down the stairs of his silent house, and made his way to the south-side balcony on the second floor. Kanai appeared at the landing of the staircase, rubbing his eyes with his knuckles. He stifled a yawn when he saw Korta babu, the man of the house, and hurried toward the kitchen.

Akhil Banerjee stood on the balcony that overlooked Uday Shankar Sarani, a quiet street away from the main road. On his left was the lush green expanse of the Royal Calcutta Golf Course. He leaned over and took a deep breath. Mothers were shouting at their children to hurry up and get ready for school. Somewhere in the distance a radio crackled to life. Headline news was followed by a jingle. The milkman dumped packets of Mother Dairy milk at the doorsteps. A goat bleated. Crows cawed. Dwellers of the *basti*, the slum lining one side of the adjoining Haripada Das Lane, queued up at the lone tube-well with plastic buckets. Smell of burnt coal from earthen ovens reached his nostrils. Stray dogs chased the newspaper boy, riding an oversized bicycle, as he threw the folded dailies over the gates. A few enthusiastic morning walkers, in kurta-pajama and keds, ambled towards the park. A mini-bus honked in the distance. Calcutta was waking up.

Kanai appeared with a cup of steaming Darjeeling tea. Akhil Banerjee took a hesitant sip, and found himself wondering what it was that retired people did. There was a bit of an open space across the main road, not more than an acre perhaps – the Sabuj Kalyan Park. This park, with its gulmohar trees and intermittent patches of grass that had turned brown due to the heat, was the only respite for the residents of Golf Garden, Uday Shankar Sarani (Old Golf Club Road). Early every morning, this park would be populated with local football enthusiasts and bodybuilders. A solitary bench would be occupied by 'retirees', quintessential Bengalis with receding hairlines and protruding bellies, engaged in arguments over topics ranging from politics to the price of shrimps in the market. Akhil Banerjee saw them almost every morning during his daily walks. Why these men couldn't walk while they talked – whatever it was that they talked about, he could never tell. Sometimes they would raise a hand to acknowledge him, and if he was close enough they would invite him to join them.

'Arrey, Joj Saheb, you are quite fit, you needn't exercise everyday,' they would call out. Akhil Banerjee would politely refuse and carry on with his walk. A little exercise never hurt anyone, he would mutter under his breath.

He finished his cup of tea, and got dressed, put on his sneakers, and stepped out of his house. The air was crisp and oddly refreshing for a July day. Sounds of young boys playing football reached his ears, even before the Sabuj Kalyan Park came into full view. He decided to walk along the perimeter as usual, making a conscious effort to go behind the park bench that was now occupied by two men, the backs of whose near-balding heads glistened in the early morning sun. Akhil Banerjee completed one round with ease. As he neared the bench, he half expected an invitation and almost could not avoid looking at the twosome.

'Good morning, Joj Saheb,' called out Chandan Mukherjee, raising his hand. Akhil Banerjee, greeted them in similar fashion, and walked on. Something about the greeting felt good. He was still 'Joj Saheb' or 'Judge Sahib' to many, and no retirement was going to take that away from him. He completed his ten rounds, and approached the bench, wiping sweat off his face. The two men moved sideways to create space for him.

'Joj Saheb, you are now part of our fraternity,' said Bibhuti Bose good-humouredly. 'Welcome to retirement!'

★

Golf Garden is an old locality, with rows of one-two-or three-storey houses, separated by moss-covered boundary walls, along which creepers like ivy and bougainvillea had found refuge. The houses, far from holding any architectural interest, were conspicuous by their lack of anything not strictly utilitarian. They were simple brick structures, that rose often, right on the edge of the road, the entrances of which were guarded by wrought-iron grills or collapsible gates that jarred open anytime a visitor arrived.

There was always something inexplicably comforting about neighbourhoods of this sort. You met the same people everyday, in shops and in markets, at the bus stops or in the hair-cutting saloon. In this respect, it was not much different from any other locality, perhaps. But the comfort came from an assurance that these people – the ones you saw everyday, were not going to leave. The *paara* would remain the same, unvaryingly so, over the years. Such localities in Calcutta were rare these days. Builders and promoters pounced at every opportunity to demolish old houses and erect towering multi-storied buildings. Restless young professionals rented the pigeon-holes, moved houses, and even cities, with alarming alacrity. In such neighbourhoods, neighbours remained strangers, and one's attachment to a locality or a home was considered foolish sentimentalism.

Akhil Banerjee, being a prominent figure, was well-known to all in his *paara*. But his demanding official responsibilities, had denied him the pleasure of getting well acquainted with his neighbours. The few minutes of *adda*, with fellow retirees the day before, had been surprisingly pleasant. And he saw no harm in these indulgences every now and then.

Adda – if ever there was an activity that so completely captured the culture of a place, it was this. To describe *adda* as small talk or gossip would be to attenuate its true essence. *Adda* is not as small as small talk and not as frivolous as gossip. The topics of an *adda*, more often than not, bordered on the impersonal – politics, cinema, theatre, sports, and of course, food. It is an involved discussion, a free-flowing river of thoughts, ideas and opinions. The films of Satyajit babu and Jean-Luc Godard, Marxist philosophy and capitalism, the best biryani restaurant in Calcutta – one could hear it all in one single *adda* session. Arguments, though common, were rarely of a personal nature. If you had a strong opinion of one political party, then come election time, sparks were bound to fly. Points of view were defended, questions were raised, and challenges were made. The *addas* of Coffee House were legendary, where philosophers, artists, bureaucrats, students of the university, had heated debates over unending cups of coffee and innumerable cigarettes. In that respect, Bengalis were similar to the French. Were it not the smoke-filled cafes of Champs-Elysées and Montmartre, that had been the hotbed of debates and discussions of thinkers like Sartre and Zola, the artists like Gauguin, Van Gogh and Seurat?

Most importantly, and here lay a crucial difference with other discussions of the trivial sort – one chose to indulge in an *adda*. Phrases like 'Let me go have an adda with so and so' were common in a Bengali household. *Adda* was what the 'intellectual' Bengali thrived on, though, of course, it was not a prerogative of the cognoscenti. In that too, Bengalis were much like the French.

'Did you watch the East Bengal match yesterday, moshai?' Chandan Mukherjee's voice became audible as Akhil Banerjee neared the bench the following day.

'How can you watch these league matches after the World Cup, Chandan babu?' asked Bibhuti Bose with mild disgust. 'Our undernourished players, look like a bunch of drenched crows running helter-skelter . . . you call that football?!'

'Whatever you say, moshai . . . Prodeep Bhanja. . . .'

'*Arrey dur*, moshai, Prodeep Bhanja! Hasn't learnt the basics of football, and he gives expert commentary on ESPN.'

'It is unfair to compare our players with Latin American or European ones, don't you think, Bibhuti babu?' asked Akhil Banerjee. 'I think it has to do with the genetic make-up. Even if you gave our players the best facilities and coaching, do you think anyone would ever be a Zico or a Pele?' He shook his head.

'You are right, Joj Saheb,' said Chandan Mukherjee. 'I think our generation is so fortunate to have witnessed the likes of Pele, Vava, Didi, Garrincha, the Giants of Brazil! Nowadays football is so commercialized. The purity of the game is no longer there, don't you think?'

'True, Brazilian football is a class apart,' agreed Bibhuti Bose. 'But in my opinion, the greatest footballer the world has seen does not come from that country.'

'Really? Who do you mean, Bibhuti babu?'

'Why, Maradona, of course! Don't you remember the goal against England, World Cup '86? Who has even come close to that genius, moshai?'

'No, moshai,' disagreed Chandan Mukherjee. 'I still think Pele is still better than Mara . . .'

'Ah, here comes Chaar Padabi,' announced Bibhuti Bose. Akhil Banerjee looked up to find a smiling Debdas Guha Roy approaching the bench. The significance of his nick-name 'Chaar Padabi' or 'the four surnames', invented undoubtedly by Bibhuti Bose himself, would be lost to someone not familiar with Bengali nomenclature. Considering that Deb, Das, Guha and Roy were all distinct Bengali surnames, the nickname was apt.

'How come you're late today, Debdas babu?' asked Chandan Mukherjee, as they moved sideways to create space for the new arrival.

'Got up late, moshai.'

'Debdas babu,' said Bibhuti Bose, 'we were having a discussion about who is the greatest footballer of all times. Who do you think it is? Pele or Maradona?'

'Pele, of course!' replied Debdas Guha Roy without hesitation. 'When it comes to football, it's always Brazil, and when it comes to cricket, it's always West Indies. If your loyalties lie elsewhere, you cannot be called a true Bengali, moshai,' he laughed.

'Its funny how we get so emotional over the sports of other nations,' said Akhil Banerjee. 'Arnab, when he was young, would start crying if Brazil lost a match or if Socrates missed a penalty shot! You see all these young boys of the neighbourhood clubs? Come football season, they'll paint portraits of Brazilian players on the walls, garland their posters, even break a coconut in front of the TV set before the start of the match. I have seen *paaras* being decorated with blue and yellow flags and young boys going around sporting yellow T-shirts to show their solidarity with Brazil. Yet when I visited Sao Paolo, some years ago, and mentioned this to the locals, do you know what they said?'

'What, what?'

'Where is Calcutta?'

They laughed aloud. Debdas Guha Roy shook his head, as if to say 'Unbelievable', and motioned the tea-stall boy for four cups of tea.

'It's good that you have joined us today, Joj Saheb. We finally complete the series,' he said.

He responded to the quizzical glances with a look of suppressed amusement, like a child who knows a secret that his friends do not.

'What do you mean by that, Debdas babu?'

Debdas Guha Roy took his time to answer, relishing every moment. 'Only, that all these days we were Bibhuti, Chandan, and Debdas, that is B, C and D. Now we have the A. A for Akhil babu.' He beamed with delight, as comprehension dawned on his fellow park-benchers.

'Good one, Debdas babu, good one. And now let's drink tea to that.'

An Invitation

Akhil Banerjee settled down in his armchair, on the second-floor balcony as Subhadra, poured out their tea. He struggled to spread out a copy of *The Statesman* and then fold it again to the desired section, the ceiling fan whirring right above him thwarting all his efforts. He succeeded eventually, pinning down the daily with his elbows and glanced through the headlines. The same old issues surfaced everyday – war, corruption, political propaganda. He noticed a small article titled 'High Court Judge Retires' and read it out to his wife. The two of them sat contentedly, munching Marie biscuits dipped in steaming cups of Darjeeling tea.

'Korta babu, this has come for you.' Kanai appeared with a white envelope. 'The sahib at number 12 sent you this.'

Akhil Banerjee tore it open to find a neat, handwritten invitation to Mr Agarwal's that very evening. In honour of Judge Akhil Banerjee, it said.

He pondered over the invitation. He had no intention of spending his retired life attending social gatherings he had so despised all his life. The previous evening's 'felicitations' organized by the boys of Sabuj Kalyan Samiti, with the innumerable garlands, and unending speeches by some of the prominent members of this neighbourhood and a political aspirant or two (whom Akhil Banerjee had never seen before), had been torture enough. And already here was another invitation.

While he had met Mr Agarwal several times on the street, and they had always exchanged pleasantries during those meetings, this gesture certainly seemed a little overt. But it would be awkward to turn it down, especially since it was presumably in his honour. Kanai waited expectantly for a reply, his back arched slightly, eyes on the floor, palms joined together.

'Tell him I'll be there,' sighed Akhil Banerjee, wondering how many more of these he would have to endure – well-meaning friends, relatives, colleagues, who, in an attempt to perhaps 'ease' his transition to another phase of life, only harp the same message over and over again.

'Very well, korta babu.' Kanai gathered the finished cups of tea and turned to leave.

'Oh, Kanai. . . .'

'Korta babu?'

'Could you get me the cordless phone from downstairs?'

'The phone line is dead, Korta babu,' replied Kanai. 'Since the storm two days ago . . . I have already lodged a complaint.'

'Oh, I see. Never mind then.' Akhil Banerjee returned to the paper.

★

The rickshaw carrying Bibhuti Bose swung into Uday Shankar Sarani with lightning speed, managing to barely avoid a couple of boys running after a ball.

'*Horn kyon nahin bajata hain*?' yelled Bibhuti Bose tightening his grip on the handle. The rickshaw-wallah pretended not to hear him, and sped on.

'*Roko, hum idhar girega*,' called out Bibhuti Bose.

'*Arrey, kyon girega*, babu? *Aap kaskey pakariye na*,' replied the rickshaw-wallah.

'Uff! *Hum idhar hi girega. Samajhta nahin, bewakoof! Mera ghar peechey reh gaya*.'

'Oh, ho,' said the rickshaw-wallah as he wheeled around. '*Girega, kyon boltey hain babu, utrega boliye na*'.

Misunderstandings of this nature occurred frequently with Bibhuti Bose. But these failed to discourage him from rattling off in Hindi with rickshaw-pullers and taxi-drivers, automatically assumed to hail from the neighbouring Hindi speaking state of Bihar. For his wife, Joyoti Bose, frustration would at times surpass all limits. When already late for an invitation or an appointment, their taxi would be going round and round in circles unable to locate the address, thanks to her husband's directions dispensed in Hindi. 'Why won't you speak to him in Bengali?' she would thunder. 'They have come to work here; don't you think their Bengali would be better than your Hindi?'

Women! Bibhuti Bose would muse. What did they know of the ways of the world? The taxi-driver had perfectly understood his directions, but was just pretending to be lost, as this would ensure a higher fare on his already tampered meter. Bibhuti Bose would show him, as soon as they reached their destination; if they reached their destination.

Now, getting off the rickshaw with some effort, he grumbled about mentally-challenged Bihari rickshaw-wallahs, paid the fare in loose change and ambled towards his home, a bulging nylon bag in each arm.

'They have the freshest Ilish in the market today,' he called out as he lowered the bags on to the floor.

Bibhuti Bose had retired a year ago from the post of General Manager of a British multinational, BOC India Ltd. (often jocularly called Bunch of Criminals by rival companies, but which the company management had reasserted as Best Operating Company). He was shorter than the average Bengali. His oversized paunch stuck out from his otherwise thin frame. He had wavy gray and black hair, and a thin moustache. His oval face was deeply tanned and his lips were almost permanently tainted red, from the constant chewing of betel leaves or *paan*. His accent was unmistakably East Bengali, a remnant of his early days spent in Dhaka, a fact he would be reminded of over and over again during his numerous applications for jobs, loans, and more recently a passport; Place of birth: Dhaka (now in Bangladesh) or Dhaka (in erstwhile India).

Joyoti Bose came out of the kitchen, wiping her turmeric stained fingers on the loose end of her sari. There were few things in the world that brought ecstatic joy in the lives of Bibhuti and Joyoti Bose. 'Ilish *maachch*' or Hilsa fish was easily number one on the list. Roshogolla, a soft, white, spongy paneer ball dripping with sugary syrup, was a close second.

Joyoti Bose had just taken out the two-kilogram fish from the bag, and was eyeing it with profound adoration, when the doorbell sounded. A Nepali Bahadur, a watchman, stood just beyond the iron grill, and gave a curt 'Shalam Shaab', before handing Bibhuti Bose a white envelope.

'Mr Agarwal has invited us tonight,' called out Bibhuti Bose to his wife, who had already disappeared into the kitchen, and was giving quick instructions to the maid on how to cook the fish.

'Agarwal?' asked Joyoti Bose, the name apparently not ringing a bell.

'Yes, at number 12. Says he is giving a party in honour of Joj Saheb. Didn't know they were close. . . .'

'Oh, Number 12? You mean the non-Bengali gentleman who lives in the house diagonally across? He always speaks so loudly on the phone, doesn't he? What time is the party?'

Bibhuti Bose glanced through the invitation.

'Does it say "Mr Bose and family"?' continued his wife. 'Wonder if Chhaya di will be going. Must find out what she'll be wearing. Cannot afford to repeat what happened at Abani Babu's grandson's thread ceremony. Do you remember? Both Chhaya di and I had worn almost identical saris. Everyone kept saying we looked like sisters. It was so awkward, really. Should I give your kurta-pajama for a wash?'

Bibhuti Bose did not dare interrupt the soliloquy, wondering the best way to break the news.

'Umm,' he mumbled eventually, 'It doesn't say anything about "family". I think it is just us gentlemen.'

Joyoti Bose stepped out of the kitchen and stole a glance at the Bahadur who seemed determined not to look her way. She stormed out of the room, raising her voice a few decibels higher than was strictly required.

'I say, Subala, are you done cleaning the fish yet, or will I have to wait for another year to eat it?'

★

Chandan Mukherjee stepped out of his bath in a red and white chequered towel tied tightly around his waist, droplets of water trickling down his body. Muttering the hymns of Goddess Kali, he squeezed water out of the long narrow white threads – the symbol of his high Brahmin caste, which hung crossbow from his shoulder.

Chandan Mukherjee had retired a few years ago from the State Bank of India. His balding head and frequent use of a walking stick, which he insisted was necessary due to his arthritic pains, made him look much older than he really was. He considered himself a *pucca* Bengali. He would rarely step out of the house in anything other than a *dhuti-panjabi.* He believed strongly in preserving everything that made Bengal great; the walls in his house were decorated with portraits of Bengali stalwarts of yesteryears – Netaji, Swami Vivekananda and Tagore. The music that emanated from his house was Rabindra sangeet or Shyama sangeet, the smell that wafted from his kitchen was of *mocha, ghonto,* lentils tempered with asafoetida and fish fried in mustard oil. He could never fathom how his sons could have an entire meal of 'pizza', rubbery bread smothered with ketchup and cheese.

'Maa Bhabani . . . arrey somebody get the door. . . .' He hollered between his chants as the door bell sounded. 'Korunamoyi. . . .'

Still dripping, he came down the stairs taking support of the banister. His flip-flops left watery stains on the red-cemented steps. On the way to the main door, he stopped at the ground floor kitchen to see if the maid was in.

'What, Protima? Couldn't you hear the doorbell?'

'How can I hear it, Dadababu? It's not possible to hear the sound of my own voice with this machine.' She pointed to the exhaust fitted snugly above the gas burner.

'Where is Boudi?'

'In the bathroom downstairs.'

The doorbell sounded again.

'I'm coming, I'm coming,' he called out.

He took the white envelope from the Bahadur, his brows knitted in suspicion. He was sure he had never seen this person before.

'What is this?' he asked. It was one of those questions that Bahadur thought was pointless to answer.

Chandan Mukherjee tore open the envelope and pored through its contents.

'What is this?' he asked again, as if unable to comprehend what he had just read. This time the question needed answering, thought Bahadur.

'Shaab has asked few gentlemen to his house this evening,' he said, hoping he had made the meaning clearer.

'Yes, yes, I can see that, but *iye*. . . .' *Iye* was a word often used by Chandan Mukherjee. It was not really so much a word, as it was a word-substitute. Whenever he failed to come up with an appropriate term, it was always replaced with *iye*. In social situations of extreme stress, such as this, *iye* also had the power to usurp whole sentences altogether.

'Who is Mr Agarwal? I don't really *iye* him.'

Bahadur wonders, *iye* meaning?? Know? Like? Fancy?

'Shaab, he is the shaab at number 12, the big white house down the road.'

'I see, but why does he want to *iye* me?'

Invite, see, befriend?

'Shaab is giving big party for Juj Shaab. Everybody is coming, including Juj Shaab.' Bahadur thought it best to stress the last point, sensing that this particular invitee seemed a little slow to grasp the gist.

'Hmm, but it is awfully short *iye*.'

Bahadur was stumped. He thought he had been mentally filling in the blanks fairly correctly up until now, but *awfully short what? Letter, notice?*

'Party's only in the evening, shaab,' he hastened. 'Plenty of time. . . .'

'Okay.'

Bahadur lingered a second or two longer at the threshold, unsure if the 'Okay' was a dismissal or a confirmation or both. But it didn't look like this Shaab was going to offer any more clues. He did a 'Shalam Shaab' and hurried off to the next house.

★

Debdas Guha Roy sat cross-legged on the living room divan, managing to crease the floral bedcover just a little.

He had been a professor of geology at Ashutosh College. The college, one of the oldest in Calcutta, had been founded by Sir Ashutosh Mukherjee, and had seen glorious days in the past. In recent times, its credit lay in producing several first classes or distinctions, by students labelled 'not brilliant enough' by the more prestigious institutes.

Debdas Guha Roy took pride in his teaching. To the average person, his subject was not as glamorous as physics or mathematics, and one rarely studied geology out of sheer passion for rocks and the like. More often than not, it was a 'Pass Subject', which, one merely had to pass, to fulfil the degree requirements. He would often reflect on the unfortunate state of the country's education system, where an insane compulsion forced every high school student to pursue engineering or medicine, irrespective of their inherent inclinations. Those were the degrees that assured good jobs. Not literature, not the social sciences, and certainly not geology! Many students, who failed to secure a seat in the engineering or medical colleges would renounce the sciences after high school and opt for accountancy instead, as this too assured a better chance of getting employment. How could mere placing of numbers in columns and adding them up, be more exciting than the study of two chemicals mingling in a test tube to produce entirely different products? Or the study of an atom, the very substance we are made of? A tiny, positive charge engulfed in a cloud of electrons, yet by their very act of coming together, by their arranging themselves in an unseen, unknown predestined order, creating solid shapes as hard as rocks and mountains. Did one of them even stop to ponder on this? And what about language and literature? How often did Bengalis, their heads held high with obvious pride, proclaim that Rabindranath was one of them, that Ishwar Chandra Vidyasagar was their own, as were Sarat Chandra and Bankim Chandra? Yet, how many parents encouraged their children to study Bengali literature, let alone pursue it as a career? These very parents, who helped their children write eloquent essays on India's freedom struggle, the many sacrifices and acts of bravery of our sons, would now coax them to converse in English, even at the expense of learning very little of their mother tongue. Are we really free from British rule? Freedom . . . it was such an illusion.

And what about geology, the study of the earth? The home of all our ancestors and the billions of exotic and wondrous species, some extinct, some endangered, others surviving in a delicately balanced eco-system that threatened to fall apart at the slightest callousness? How would engineers build rail-roads, bridges, and monuments without the knowledge of geological sciences? It was knowledge of the very earth we walked on! From the study of fossils and dinosaur bones, volcanoes and earthquakes, climate change and drilling for oil, there was hardly an area where knowledge of geology was not applied. Really, when one thought of it, there couldn't possibly be another subject as fascinating as this!

But all this had not deterred him from trying hard to infuse enthusiasm in his students. He taught with passion. And honesty. Once, his daughters, Piya and Diya, had given him a hand-drawn greeting card for his birthday. With sparkly paint and stencils, they had written the words 'Geology Rocks!' on it. He had spent the better part of the day arguing that the sentence was incomplete. Should it not have been something like, geology is the study of rocks? Why would anyone want to put a definition on a card, his daughters argued. 'Rocks' here is a verb, they explained. This only made matters worse, as this particular verb did not appear anywhere in the long list of verbs in the dog-eared *Wren and Martin* grammar book that Debdas Guha Roy had fished out from his library. He had wondered aloud about the appalling condition of education these days. It was only days later, when one of his best students had eyed the card and remarked 'Cool!' that an inkling of doubt had cropped up in Debdas Guha Roy's mind. Perhaps *Wren and Martin* had been replaced by more advanced grammar books.

Now, reaching for a robust oversized pillow behind his back, and placing it on his lap, he eyed the weary foursome seated on the floor before him. What a tragic sight, he thought. Teenagers, still in high school, yet one look at their faces and you knew that life had already been sucked out of them. For several years now, their daily routine was, home to school, school to tuitions, back home for dinner, and then off to bed. Where was the time to play or pursue other interests? Where would one play? Who would one play with? Tragic!

He took out several xeroxed sheets from a file, and evened them out on the pillow. The students opened a fresh page in their notebooks, unhurriedly, without the slightest eagerness to absorb the knowledge that would now be given unto them. The knowledge that would help them earn those extra marks in their board exams, and for which, their parents have unabashedly usurped their Sunday morning cricket matches in the by-lanes.

He was just about to start with the day's topic, igneous rocks, when Diya's voice interrupted him.

'Baba?' she called out from behind the yellow and white striped curtain that hung precariously over the green enamel door.

'What is it?'

'This has come for you.' An outstretched arm, carrying a white envelope, made its way into the room through the folds of the curtain. The students, whose tired faces had lit up momentarily in the hope of catching a glimpse of their teacher's daughter, soon went back to normal, when Debdas Guha Roy took the envelope from the arm, and the arm (with the rest of his daughter) retracted into the forbidden quarters of their home.

In Honour of Juj Saab

Mr Agarwal's living room was elegantly furnished, with two large sofas facing each other, and several beautifully handcrafted wooden chairs upholstered in fine fabric. The room had two pairs of tall windows, in the east and in the south. An ornate wooden cabinet filled with various artefacts stood against the south wall. Old paintings of *maharajas* and battle scenes adorned the north wall.

'This is true aristocracy, moshai,' whispered Chandan Mukherjee to Bibhuti Bose.

The two of them had been shown in by Bikash Bakshi, Mr Agarwal's secretary. They seated themselves on one of the sofas and glanced about the room in admiration.

'Yes, a true man of taste,' Bibhuti Bose agreed.

Mr Agarwal came in shortly, smiling broadly, palms pressed together in a 'Namaskar'. He was short and heavy, with a round face and shaggy eyebrows. He wore round gold-rimmed spectacles, and a pair of golden teeth sparkled as he smiled. He was dressed in a starched white kurta and *chost*.

'This is such an honour, gentlemen,' said Mr Agarwal in heavily accented Bengali as he motioned them to sit.

Akhil Banerjee, Dr Subodh Mullick and Debdas Guha Roy arrived shortly after.

'I see you have a very interesting collection, Mr Agarwal,' said Akhil Banerjee, once everyone was seated. 'It must have taken you years to collect these?'

The host smiled humbly. 'What can I say Juj Saab? I have been quite lucky.

My great-grandfather, Ram Mohan Agarwal was the Diwan of the Maharajah of Pithorgarh. He had been a collector in his time. I suppose you can say that this hobby runs in our veins. When it was time for his retirement, he asked the Maharajah for some unique items. This hukka, for example, the Maharajah himself used to smoke on this beauty. Some of the paintings too are from that era.'

'They must be worth quite a lot,' the words escaped Debdas Guha Roy's mouth, before he could stop himself. But thankfully, Mr Agarwal did not seem to mind. He simply smiled humbly.

Refreshments had been laid on the table and conversation flowed easily. The guests allowed their eyes to drift from one object to another.

'Shaab, *aapsey koi milney aaya hain.*' (Someone's here to see you), announced Bahadur, stepping into the room.

'Who is it?'

'Says he has an appointment?'

'Oh ho!' said Mr Agarwal, slapping his forehead. 'I completely forgot. I'm really sorry, gentlemen. I had an appointment with a seller of curio items.' He hesitated. 'It would be unfair to send him away . . . But. . . .'

'*Arrey* no, no,' protested the guests. 'Please keep your appointment, Mr Agarwal.'

'Okay, send him in.'

Presently a thin man, probably in his early thirties, entered hesitantly. He wore a pale blue shirt and khaki trousers. His long face was amply covered with a beard and a moustache.

'I apologize,' he said to the man, motioning him to take a seat 'Mr. . . . ?'

'Hazra. Sujit Hazra.'

'Yes, Mr Hazra. I'm sorry I completely forgot about our appointment. I have invited Juj Saab and some friends. Please show me what you have brought. I may not be able to give you an answer immediately.'

'Alright,' said Sujit Hazra. He fished out some items from his cloth bag; an ashtray, a smoking pipe, a mirror. Mr Agarwal held them under the lamp, and examined them carefully.

'You say these belong to Lord Clive?' he asked.

'Y . . . yess.'

Mr Agarwal shook his head. 'Don't look like 18th century pieces . . . Where did you find them?'

'I've always had them. I guess they belonged to one of my ancestors.' His voice was soft, and it trembled slightly when he spoke.

Mr Agarwal brought the pipe close to his eyes, squinted, pushing up his spectacles as he did so.

'Mr Hazra,' he said, handing the items back, 'when it comes to historical pieces, it's very important to do thorough research. Take a look at all these items . . .' He indicated the artefacts all around. 'One hundred per cent genuine stuff. Gentlemen, let me show you something . . .' He left the room. Sujit Hazra fidgeted nervously with the buttons of his shirt. After a while he stood up, ready to leave, but just then Mr Agarwal returned. Sujit Hazra hesitated, unsure of whether or not to stay, but decided to sit down again.

Mr Agarwal held a small velvet box in his hand. His guests leaned forward to take a better look. As he popped open the box, the guests let out a suppressed gasp. In the box, was a brilliant diamond, the size of an oversized grape!

He passed the box around. 'Belonged to the late Maharani of the Garhwals,' he informed everyone. 'You see? A genuine historical piece . . . My late wife had inherited it from her parents,' he said, taking the box back from Bibhuti Bose.

'Your late wife?' asked Akhil Banerjee.

Mr Agarwal nodded. 'She died under very tragic circumstances, Mr Banerjee,' he sighed.

'What happened?' asked Chandan Mukherjee.

Mr Agarwal shook his head. 'Some other day gentlemen. I wouldn't want to spoil our evening with a tragic tale of personal loss.'

'I'm sorry, Mr Agarwal,' said Akhil Banerjee. The others murmured similarly.

Mr Agarwal stared at his hands as if recollecting the memories of his tragic past in the lines that crisscrossed his palms. 'Only those who were with me at that time know what I have gone through. Anyway. . . .' he sighed, 'sooner or later, we all have to go, right?' He looked up and smiled broadly at his guests, a sad smile, but it helped to lighten the atmosphere.

'Uh . . . I have to leave,' said Mr Hazra, getting up from his seat. 'I wouldn't want to take any more of your time.'

He turned around, a little too hastily, lost his balance and tripped over. The contents of his cloth bag spilled out. Bibhuti Bose and Debdas Guha Roy hastened to help him. Sujit Hazra gathered his belongings, mumbled a hurried apology and left.

'Is that a Jamini Roy?' asked Akhil Banerjee, pointing to the painting of a young Santhal girl.

'You seem to know art well, Juj Saab!' Mr Agarwal's cheery disposition had returned and he spoke animatedly. 'Yes, I have always been a big admirer of Bengali artists . . . Jamini Roy, Nandalal Bose, Ramkinkar . . . I was very lucky to have secured that one. These days, good Indian art is no longer within the reach of ordinary folks.'

Akhil Banerjee walked up to the painting.

'Are you sure it is safe to leave it in your house like this? I mean, without proper protection? You should probably keep it in a bank locker, no?' said Debdas Guha Roy.

Mr Agarwal smiled. 'How many people know the value of art, Mr Guha Roy? Most burglars would prefer to steal my Ganesh *murti*, or the hundreds of curio items lying about. They wouldn't give this painting a second glance. Besides, I like to be surrounded by my favourite things. What is the point in acquiring something with so much effort and not being able to see it everyday?'

'It is so interesting to see changes in the style of an artist, isn't it?' said Akhil Banerjee returning to his seat. 'Jamini Roy, for example, when he first started painting, his style was very European, influenced by the Impressionist paintings. Yet most people only know him for his Patua-style folk art. Same with Picasso. He used to paint figures and scenes like every other artist of his age. His Cubism came much later,' said Akhil Banerjee.

'Moshai, the thing about art is,' said Chandan Mukherjee, 'that it's really very difficult for the layman to appreciate it. Just the other day I read in the papers, a painting of squares got auctioned for millions of dollars. What is the specialty of it, tell me?'

'I agree, Chandan babu, that it is extremely difficult to appreciate art, without some proper knowledge or guidance,' said Akhil Banerjee. 'Unless you understand the thought process of the artist, or the context in which he conceived of a subject, or perhaps the various experiences that he has gone through in life, I would say, it is next to impossible to truly appreciate the value of his work. The squares that you mentioned could be an example of minimalist art. To give you an example, Piet Mondrian, the Dutch artist, started off by painting landscapes, and one day thought, why do I have to draw so many things to convey what I'm trying to say? He simply started removing all that was unnecessary, and finally was left with a few straight lines and solid colours. And that is how he is famous today.'

'Our history is filled with examples of how little, artists were understood in their times,' added Mr Agarwal. 'Take Van Gogh . . . such amazing genius! Those colours, those brushstrokes, the expressions, yet the man died a pauper.'

'And after his death, the whole world went crazy over his sunflowers and irises and potato-eaters,' said Dr Subodh Mulllick.

'Ah! Those sunflowers!' sighed Mr Agarwal. 'I tell you, doctor babu, when I stood in front of that canvas in a museum in Paris, I considered myself most fortunate. How amazing was his belief in his work that he refused to change it in order to appease those around him! He knew, he must have known, that it will be accepted one day. Unfortunately he never lived to see that day. I even visited his grave in Paris to offer my respects.'

The servant entered the room to fill the empty trays with more roasted cashews, onion fritters and sweets. Mr Agarwal was now drawing everyone's attention to a bronze wine jug that had apparently belonged to Jahangir, the Mughal Emperor.

Bibhuti Bose helped himself to a sweet. 'Is this from Tewari's, Mr Agarwal?'

'How did you know, sir?' asked Mr Agarwal surprised. 'You must really know sweet shops in Calcutta.'

'Ha ha . . . for the best non-Bengali sweets I always go to Tewari's. They also make delicious *jalebis* and *samosas*.'

'True, true. But which shop would you recommend for Bengali sweets, Mr Bose?'

'You see, the thing about Bengali sweets is that each shop has its own specialty. K.C.Dass for *roshogolla*, Jadab Das for sandesh and *mishti-doi*, Sen Mohasay for *darbesh*,' said Bibhuti Bose.

'Ganguram for *mihidana*, Shoilo Sweets for *langcha*,' added Chandan Mukherjee.

'Moshai, do you know the story of Shoilo sweets?' asked Debdas Guha Roy.

'What story?'

'This Mr Shoilo . . . I forget his last name, was a *ghotok*, a matchmaker. He happened to be very successful in his business, and one of his clients, whose three daughters had been married off with Shoilo babu's help, offered him a sweet shop that he had owned for many years. Now Shoilo babu, took ownership of the sweet shop, and started making *langcha*. He was also a big devotee of Ma Kali. *Byas*, overnight he became a success. From that one shop he opened branches all over Calcutta.'

'When talking about sweets in Calcutta, I think the most interesting story is that of the *ledikeni*,' said Bibhuti Bose.

'Really? What story?' asked Dr Mullick.

'Don't you know? It was during the time of Lord Canning, the Viceroy. All over the settlement, every street, port, town, building was being named after him. Canning this, Canning that. Then one sweet shop owner made this round dark sweet, and named it Lady Canning. *Byas*! It became an instant hit. Calcuttans were gulping Lady Canning by the dozen.'

'Oh, you mean to say *ledikeni* is actually Lady Canning? Ha ha,' laughed Dr Mullick along with the others. 'Interesting, I never knew that.'

'But whatever you say, Mr Bose,' continued Mr Agarwal, 'in spite of Bengalis having such a passion for sweets, I am yet to find a good laddoo shop in Calcutta.'

'What are you saying Mr Agarwal? Have you not tried Sharma's?'

'Yes, yes, I have. But I tell you, if you taste the laddoos of Kanpur, you'll not want to touch these ones. My wife's family was from Kanpur . . . and the sweets they made for my wedding . . . aha ha . . . I shall never forget the taste. You see, in Kanpur, there are two shops run by two brothers; Thagoo key Laddoo and Badnaam Kulfi. You see the mischief in the names? *Thaggoo* means a 'cheat' and *badnaam* means 'one with a bad reputation'. Yet, everyone, right from the ministers in their ambassadors to businessmen in their Mercedes' would come to these shops almost daily. For any outsider visiting Kanpur, a stop at their shops is a must.'

Plates and glasses were re-filled, conversation rolled on seamlessly from one topic to another. Eventually Debdas Guha Roy looked at his watch, and announced that he should like to get going.

He had a class to take the following morning. The others got up as well, taking turns to thank their gracious host for a delightful evening. Mr Agarwal thanked each one of his guests for gracing his home.

A Theft

'*Arrey*, are you listening?' shouted Joyoti Bose for the third time. This time she raised her voice even higher and swung the morning newspaper like a baton, as if the prospect of being whacked on the head by this domestic instrument would somehow enter Bibhuti Bose's subconscious mind, and wake him up to reality. It might have even worked, for Bibhuti Bose stopped snoring, stirred a little, half opened his eyes and in that slurry voice that suggested that he was not quite awake yet, managed to ask 'What happened?'

'What happened you ask? Robbery, dacoity! Right under your nose!'

Bibhuti Bose sat up. 'What are you saying, Joyoti? Dacoity? Where?'

'Look at the morning paper. First column under Local news. Mr Agarwal's diamond was stolen last night.'

Bibhuti Bose put on his spectacles and grabbed the newspaper from his wife. He became aware of his faster heartbeat, as he hurriedly turned the pages to the desired section.

'"Priceless diamond stolen"' he read the article aloud, his brows knitted in an effort to concentrate, as Joyoti Bose supplied live breaking news of the neighbourhood.

'"Late last night a very rare diamond ring was stolen from Mr Agarwal's home in Golf Garden."'

'Police was here last night and even this morning. They questioned all the servants. You better brush your teeth and wear something nice . . . they will surely want to question you too,' said Joyoti Bose.

'"Mr Agarwal had earlier invited some local residents to his house, most notably the Retd. Judge Akhil Banerjee, and had shown the diamond to all his guests. The disappearance was noticed almost immediately after the guests left. He instantly notified the police who searched and questioned the servants. Nothing was found. The diamond was said to have belonged to the late Queen of Garhwal."'

'Did you see anything last night? *Tell me na.* You have to tell the police everything, so try to remember very well. This is so exciting . . . everyone from the *dhobi*'s son to the rickshaw pullers are talking about it.'

'The police are on the look-out for a Sujit Hazra, who had also been to Mr Agarwal's house that evening on the pretext of selling curio items. Inspector Sudarshan Rakshit was quoted saying, "We are doing everything to catch the thief at the earliest".'

'Who do you think did it?'

'My god!' exclaimed Bibhuti Bose as he put down the paper. Ignoring his wife's unending questions, he rushed to the telephone in the living room.

It was answered after three rings.

'Have you seen *The Statesman*, Chandan babu?'

'Arrey, Bibhuti babu, who needs to read the papers for news like this? We heard it first from the milkman this morning. Then at the park this is all everyone was talking about. Why didn't you join us today?'

'I couldn't sleep last night, Chandan babu. Took a couple of Valium tablets late in the night, so couldn't get up early. So what do you think happened?'

'Listen moshai; let's not discuss these things over the phone. The police have already been to Joj Saheb's house and to Dr Mullick's as well. They will come over to our homes surely.' Bibhuti Bose heard a faint female voice instructing Chandan Mukherjee. 'I'm going, I'm going,' answered Chandan Mukherjee to the voice. 'My wife forgot to mention 'green chillies', moshai. Have to go to the market again. Let's cooperate the best we can . . . though you know how these things are. The police are rarely successful in cases like these.'

'Yes, yes I understand.' Bibhuti Bose hung up. 'Talk to you later.'

★

Akhil Banerjee stepped out of his house, and instantly felt the heat scorching his skin. He pushed open the umbrella and made his way towards the STD/PCO booth at the corner of Ghulam Mohammed Shah Road and Uday Shankar Sarani. Balai, the owner of the PCO booth looked up disinterestedly from the Bengali daily, and immediately hastened to free a plastic chair of old magazines. He dusted the chair with the newspaper roll, and offered it to Akhil Banerjee.

'Phone's busy, sir,' he sounded apologetic. 'You might have to wait a while. . . .'

'No problem,' said Akhil Banerjee, as he settled down on the chair.

The air was hot and humid. Drops of sweat surfaced on his face and neck. The mini-buses on the main road honked loudly, and blew heavy clouds of exhaust as they went past. A quarrel had ensued amongst two rickshaw-wallahs over who was rightfully next in line. Akhil Banerjee felt a throbbing start inside his head, and he looked impatiently at the man who was still inside the booth.

'Will it be long?' he asked Balai.

'Ah . . . sir . . . let me see.'

Balai tapped on the glass door, pushed it open and thrust his head inside. After a few seconds of muffled conversation, he turned to face Akhil Banerjee. 'STD call sir, to Kanpur. Just a couple of minutes more, he says.'

'Alright.'

Eventually the door of the booth opened.

'Arrey, Mr Bakshi?' asked Akhil Banerjee. 'Didn't realize it was you.'

Bikash Bakshi hesitated as if unable to place the face.

'Oh, Joj Saheb? I didn't know you were waiting. Had I known I would have definitely. . . .'

'No, no . . . its alright,' replied Akhil Banerjee. 'How's Mr Agarwal doing? It's so shocking what happened last night.'

Bikash Bakshi shook his head.

'He is naturally very disturbed. A thing like this has never happened before to him, you see. How I regret not being there when it happened. Normally Mr Agarwal gives me the Sunday evenings off. I showed you all to the living room, and then left to catch a show at Bhabani cinema. I returned home late to find the police questioning the servants.'

'Hmm . . . how long have you been Mr Agarwal's secretary?'

'Almost five years now, ever since he moved to this locality.'

'And you live in Mr Agarwal's house as well?'

'Yes, on the ground floor. It's a fairly nice arrangement. If I had to rent a place on my own, I wouldn't have had any money to save, to send back to my mother.'

'True, true . . . hmm . . . I suppose Mr Agarwal's phone line is dead too?'

'Huh? Oh yes, what with the storm and everything . . . God knows how long it will take to repair the lines this time.'

'Please tell him that I'm really sorry about what happened and that I would like to drop by later today to have a word with him?'

'Of course, sir.'

A middle aged lady in a cotton printed sari made her way to the STD booth.

'Joj Saheb was here first,' said Balai stopping her.

'Where?' asked the lady. 'Was he in line? I didn't see him in line.'

Balai ignored her and gently shoved Akhil Banerjee inside the booth. 'Please sir, this way,' he said solicitously.

'Good day, sir,' called out Bikash Bakshi. 'I will tell Mr Agarwal to expect you today.'

★

The Daily Market was bustling with people as usual. Vendors sat on coarse jute carpets, spread out on the sidewalk. Stalls had been built with tarpaulin roofs supported by four bamboo pillars. Vegetables of the same kind had been grouped together. They were now being weighed in a hand-balance and being poured into the customers' bags. Prices were being negotiated and then rounded off. If it was the day's first sale, the crisp notes would be placed briefly on the forehead and a quick prayer would be muttered, before the money disappeared under the jute carpet.

Bibhuti Bose was loyal to only one vegetable vendor, only one fruit seller and only one fishmonger. If Jadu, Bishu and Nimai (as were their respective names) did not have the bitter gourd or yam that his wife had insisted upon, then it was not in Bibhuti Bose to ignore his loyalty and go searching for these items under the next tarpaulin shed. In fact, so absolute was his trust in Jadu, Bishu and Nimai, that he would simply drop off his nylon sack along with Joyoti Bose's list, at the respective stalls, and then wander off to complete the other errands of the day. The errands, which mostly consisted of paying his corporation tax, or the telephone and electricity bills, or a visit to the bank or the post office, usually ended with a visit to the local paan shop. Paan was betel leaf smeared with red and white pastes and sprinkled with a flavoured 'Baba Zarda'. He would then return to collect his nylon bags, now filled with wares corresponding to his wife's list.

It would be too much to say however, that Jadu, Bishu and Nimai had always acted in a manner that had assured them of Bibhuti Bose's loyalty towards them. Ever so often, Joyoti Bose would encounter a rotten brinjal or an unripe mango. Bibhuti Bose would assure her that the matter would be properly dealt with the next day. But Joyoti Bose knew better. It would take a lot more than a couple of rotten vegetables a week to drive her husband's loyalty elsewhere.

'They must be calling you Pocha Babu at the market,' she would say looking at a particularly uninviting piece of fruit. 'There comes Pocha babu, they say. Let's take out all the rotten vegetables of the week which no one else has bought, and stuff them into his bag.'

This particular Monday had not been much different. Bibhuti Bose having entrusted his nylon sacks to the vendors and having completed his trip to the Allahabad Bank, Golf Garden branch, had just placed an order for a paan, when he spotted Chandan Mukherjee.

'*Arrey* moshai, we are all celebrities now. What do you say?' he called out.

Chandan Mukherjee coughed politely. 'Just being mentioned in the paper does not give us celebrity status, Bibhuti babu.'

'Both *Ananda Bazar* and *Statesman* have covered it. Now I hear a crew from the channel 'Khas Khabar' will also be coming to interview us. Once the word gets out, there's no stopping moshai, you wait and see.'

'Yes, I see what you mean. But I don't think this matter should be given any undue importance. After all. . . .'

'What are you saying, moshai? A rare diamond ring gets stolen right from under the Judge's nose, and it's not important? Its sensational, moshai . . . simply sensational!'

They ambled to the vegetable section of the market. All around them, negotiations of various degrees and intensities were taking place.

'How much for that melon?'

'Ten rupees, boudi.'

'I'll give you six.'

'Eight.'

'Seven.'

'Seven and a half. No less, boudi. I bought it for more than this price.'

'Never mind the melon, then. How much for one kilo of tomatoes?'

'Arrey, Joj Saheb!' called out Chandan Mukherjee. 'How come you are at the market today? I mean, I haven't seen you here before. . . .'

'That's true,' replied Akhil Banerjee, walking towards them. 'It's Kanai, my manservant, who usually does everything. But today I had to make an urgent call, and our phone line is dead since two days. Was just returning from the STD booth, and thought of passing by the market.'

'Oh ho, I see. So what do you think happened at Mr Agarwal's? Was it one of the servants?'

'That is most likely. Though when exactly could they have managed it. . . .'

'Maybe they stole it after we left. How could they have stolen it while we were all there?' asked Bibhuti Bose.

Chandan Mukherjee shook his head. 'I called Mr Agarwal this morning,' he said. 'He says that he was all alone in the room after we left. No one else had entered. . . .'

'Really strange, moshai,' quipped Bibhuti Bose. 'Anyway, I have to get going gentlemen. Those potatoes must be getting rotten sitting in the bag.' He said a hasty goodbye and made his way home.

'Chandan babu, when did you say you called Mr Agarwal?' asked Akhil Banerjee. The two of them came out of the market and started towards home.

'*Ei toh* . . . just before coming here.'

'Hmm, that must mean his phone line was fine this morning.'

★

The evening of 8th July saw the ladies of Uday Shankar Sarani, Golf Garden (Old Golf Club Road), huddled together, deep in conversation. The sight was not an unusual one of course, for this was the time of the day best suited for exchanging local news.

Be it the secret affair of the girl in the pink churidar with the Punjabi boy of the 3rd floor, block B of Jamuna Apartments, or the reason behind the sudden sacking of Kalimoti, the housemaid of three years to Bijon Babu, one always heard it here first. If they could be just a little more proactive, they might even arrange for a club house, the sign at whose entrance would read, Golf Garden Gossipmongers Association (for women only).

That today's meeting generated a lot of excitement was evident from the raised voices and animated hand gestures.

'Agarwal babu has numerous curios,' said an easily excitable Joyoti Bose. 'Why do you think the thief took this particular item? Because Agarwal babu was. . .' 'Who are you calling "thief", Joyoti di?' interrupted Kalpana Mukherjee. 'Only our husbands were present there. No outsider, you see?'

'Arrey no no, Kalpana di, you forget the servants. They were there throughout . . . bringing in snacks, tea, *shorbot*,' clarified Joyoti Bose, with the surety of someone who had been present at the party.

Chhaya Guha Roy supported the theory. 'Those servants must be listening at the door. And there was another man who had come to sell some items. He had left much earlier of course, but who is to say he did not manage to pocket the ring before he left?

It seems Mr Agarwal drew attention to this particular piece, even naming a value for it. How can someone resist these temptations, tell me? It is but natural. In my mind. . . .'

'You are right, Chhaya,' Kalpana Mukherjee seconded. 'If it was one of the servants, he would have surely run away by now. Why would he stay on? It must have been that gentleman who had come to meet Agarwal babu. Apparently Mr Agarwal thought the items he had brought were all fake. It was just an excuse to gain entry into his house. Don't you see?'

The others nodded.

'And to think it happened in front of everybody. Not one person saw it. How strange!'

A Very Emergency Meeting

The local Club House was currently a modest shack at the end of the Sabuj Kalyan Park. Under the red-tiled roof, was a rectangular room – half of which had been occupied by a dust-covered table tennis board, a carom board and an odd assortment of sporting goods the local youth had attempted to develop an interest for. The hand-painted signboard hung atop the entrance door read Sabuj Kalyan Samiti. The name implied that members of this particular club were environment conscious, green-thumbed folks. To further strengthen this implication, the K of the Kalyan had been extended to form a leafy tree. The members of the club probably believed that an artistic representation of this sort made up for the general lack of greenery in the park, whose patches of scorched grass and couple of gulmohar trees did not do much for the club's reputation.

The mood inside the club house today was sombre. Some of the local residents had already arrived and pleasantries were being exchanged in the customary, 'Are you well?'

'What is this meeting about?' asked Bibhuti Bose, as he regarded a rickety chair with some hesitation, before finally settling on it as delicately as he could.

'I will announce shortly, kaku,' said Partho Roy, self-appointed leader of the local youth, and champion bridge player. 'I am waiting for a few more people to arrive.'

It took several minutes for those few people to arrive, as was the custom in this land. Five o'clock sharp was five fifteen on a good day. No such thing as 'sharp' when it came to time. One felt more at ease to fix the time with an – ish suffix. 'I'll see you tomorrow five-ish.' Simple and easy. No obligation on either party to arrive on time. If one met a friend on the way, and inquired after his health, and the health of his family – immediate and distant, and cursed the current rate of inflation as was evidenced by the rising cost of brinjals, and thereby arrived at the previous appointment a good half hour later, no feelings were hurt. Five o'clock, five-thirty . . . it was all the same. The government offices – one could be inclined to believe – followed highly secretive working hours that the public were purposely not made aware of. If the board outside a government office said, 10:00–12:30, and 2:00–5:00, one might arrive there at 10 o' clock 'sharp' to find the windows still closed. Windows would probably open around 11, but that in itself was no indication of when the actual work would start. A tea-break, rather a 'tea-start' would be followed by several minutes of desk clearing. And then, on a really good day, a couple of people might be entertained before the lunch break.

'Do you want to discuss the Pujo budget now?' asked Chandan Mukherjee, once everyone had settled down.

Akhil Banerjee, Bibhuti Bose, Mr Agarwal, Chandan Mukherjee, Jyoti Sen, Debdas Guha Roy, Dr Subodh Mullick, Proshanto

Sanyal, and a few of the elderly were seated in a semicircle on the chairs provided. Partho glanced over the questioning faces gathered in a semicircle around him.

'This is a very emergency meeting,' he began, his tone grave. 'There have been a few incidents in our area recently, but the latest robbery at Agarwal babu's house has been the most blatant act of crime that our *paara* has seen. This used to be a safe place, but we may have been too complacent. We cannot depend on the police. They will always arrive an hour late, and go back to the stations to play cards, and smoke *bidis*.

Now, it is up to us, the youth of today, to take pro-active steps to eliminate crime and criminals from this area. We have formed an eight-member security team here – Joy, Somen, Pinaki, Poltu, Bhombol, Jishu, Bappa and myself. We will take turns to patrol the neighbourhood at night. We ask everyone in this community to support us by contributing fifty rupees towards incidental expenses, like purchasing a few good torches, whistles and batons. Meanwhile we have a list of things that every household needs to read and follow. This is for your own safety.'

'Excellent, Partho!' exclaimed Bibhuti Bose, as the photocopies got passed around. 'If you want, we can also help. Don't underestimate us, just because we are a little, heh heh . . . but not more than two nights a week, and not beyond 11, okay?'

'Staying up late gives me gas and constipation, moshai,' he whispered to Chandan Mukherjee, seated next to him.

'Kaku, there is no need of that,' replied Partho, a wry smile on his lips. 'The thief stole the ring from right under your nose. I think the people of this neighbourhood will sleep better knowing that we, the youth, are on guard. I suggest you spend your evenings watching *saas-bahu* soap operas and leave the more serious matters to us, Kaku,' he added amidst muffled laughter amongst his friends.

A bunch of sheets were passed around, which the gathered few glanced over with varying interest.

'Iye, what is this Partho?' asked Chandan Mukherjee as he looked at his neighbours for some guidance.

'Register your maids or servants with us,' Chandan Mukherjee read aloud trying to comprehend every word. 'What is this Partho?' he asked again.

'Here, let me read it aloud for everyone,' offered Partho, as he unfolded his copy of the list.

The list was in Bengali. It read:

Register maids and servants with us (name and address).

Cost of *paara* security Rs 50 per family (for incidental expenses like torch, *lathi,* etc).

Do not talk about private matters in front of your maids, esp. your wealth, property, etc.

Keep doors locked at night.

Keep a torch.

'Partho, all this is very well . . . but our maids have all been very trustworthy. If we suddenly ask them to register their names, they might turn hostile. What if they threaten to leave?' asked Debdas Guha Roy, visibly concerned.

'Yes, yes you are right, Debdas babu. It is so hard to find a maid these days, let alone a good one,' seconded Bibhuti Bose. 'If we start questioning them, doubting them . . . as it is, most of them act so pricey. . . .'

'What if they decide to boycott us altogether? If my wife finds out about this, moshai, there will be a Kurukshetra war in my house.'

The sudden realization of the effect this news might have on their respective spouses, brought about a murmur of protests. Maids and servants were indispensable, everyone knew that. Who was going to do the dishes, wash clothes, and clean the bathrooms?

'No, no Partho, this won't do,' continued Debdas Guha Roy, encouraged by the show of support. 'The nightly patrol is fine. But I suggest you keep our maids out of this. Besides what happened at Mr Agarwal's place (very unfortunate, of course) could not possibly have been the work of any of the servants. We were all there, isn't it Mr Agarwal? We would have surely seen something?'

Mr Agarwal, who had not spoken a single word since his arrival, seemed to wake up at the mention of his name. He straightened himself in his chair, and stared hard at Debdas Guha Roy. When he spoke, his tone was grave and he took time to utter each word carefully.

'Mr Guha Roy,' he said, 'I fail to understand what you are suggesting. If it was not one of the servants, it would have to be one of the guests. And I was of the opinion that all invited were respectable gentlemen. . . .' His face had turned red, and drops of sweat formed on his forehead.

The words had an immediate effect on those present. Debdas Guha Roy opened his mouth to speak. Instead he gulped a couple of times and remained silent.

Mr Agarwal got up slowly. 'I don't think much progress can be made in this meeting, Partho,' he said. 'I wish you all a good day.'

And with those words Mr Agarwal left the room, leaving behind a dozen stunned faces.

★

'Bunch of criminals, moshai! Bunch of criminals!'

'Who are you accusing today, Bibhuti babu?' asked Akhil Banerjee, dabbing his forehead with a handkerchief. It was barely six in the morning, yet the air felt hot. A couple of hours later, even sitting under the shade of the gulmohar tree would be uncomfortable.

'Everybody, Joj Saheb. Everybody is a criminal, I tell you,' continued Bibhuti Bose animatedly. 'Did you see the way that scoundrel Partho talked to me yesterday? What audacity, moshai?'

'Ah ha! Don't take these things to heart, Bibhuti babu,' said Akhil Banerjee. 'It will only anger you more.' He fanned his face with his handkerchief. 'Wonder how long this weather will last.'

'It's all global warming, moshai,' quipped Debdas Guha Roy. 'Summers are getting hotter, monsoons are late. One doesn't even require blankets in winters these days.'

The others nodded.

'By the way, what do you gentlemen think of Mr Agarwal?' asked Akhil Banerjee presently.

'A perfect gentleman, moshai,' offered Chandan Mukherjee. 'So cultured and well-read. What a collection he has! Only a true connoisseur would be able to appreciate art like that.'

'Criminal, criminal,' muttered Bibhuti Bose under his breath.

'His outburst yesterday at the club was only natural, I think,' continued Chandan Mukherjee. 'Imagine spending a fortune in collecting valuables, and then being robbed like this. Most unfortunate, really.' He clicked his tongue.

'May be that is why he always kept to himself. He never attempted to make friends in this neighbourhood,' offered Bibhuti Bose.

'There are a lot of reasons why people keep to themselves, Bibhuti babu,' said Akhil Banerjee. 'Given that he does not like company, wouldn't you say the invitation to so many people was a bit uncharacteristic of him?'

'Joj Saheb, who do you think stole it? I mean, you have dealt with criminals all your life . . . you must have some idea, an intuition?' asked Debdas Guha Roy.

'Yes, I have been thinking about it . . . .'

'I tell you it's that Subhojit character,' offered Bibhuti Bose.

'You mean Sujit,' corrected Chandan Mukherjee.

'Subhojit, Sudip . . . it's all the same, moshai.'

'Let us just go over the facts once more shall we?' said Akhil Banerjee. 'Bibhuti babu and Chandan babu arrived first, correct?'

'Yes.'

'Hmm . . . then I arrived, followed by Dr Mullick and Debdas babu.'

'Shortly afterwards came Sujit Hazra,' said Chandan Mukherjee.

'Hmm . . . what do we know about him?' asked Akhil Banerjee.

'Sujit was there because he wanted to show Mr Agarwal some curio items,' said Debdas Guha Roy.

'Correct.'

'Do we know where he lives?'

'Baap re, Joj Saheb! You are talking like a *pucca* detective! Do you think you will be able to catch the thief?' grinned Debdas Guha Roy.

'We'll see.'

'I don't recall him mentioning anything. . . .' said Chandan Mukherjee. 'May be Mr Agarwal has his phone number?'

'No, he doesn't,' said Akhil Banerjee. 'I went to see Mr Agarwal the very next day. Apparently, Sujit Hazra had called him only a few days ago, asking for an appointment. Normally, his secretary, Bikash Bakshi, takes care of these things, but Bikash was out on an errand, and it hadn't occurred to Mr Agarwal to take down his address or phone number.'

'I tell you he is the criminal,' said Bibhuti Bose. 'Did you see the way he was acting? He spoke softly, was fidgeting the whole time . . . And that moustache and beard, I bet it was false. A disguise so that no one could recognize him later.'

'And he also left early. I suppose with the ring. What do you think, Joj Sahib?' asked Chandan Mukherjee.

'Hmm . . . it's always possible . . . How many times did we get up? I remember I got up once to see the Jamini Roy painting up close. And some of us got up to help Sujit Hazra, when he tripped. Who else got up during the evening?'

'I went out once for a smoke,' said Chandan Mukherjee. 'Was it before Mr Agarwal showed us the ring? No, I think it was after.'

'Hmm. . . .'

'And Dr Subodh Mullick excused himself once. I think Mr Agarwal showed him the way to the washroom at the end of the corridor.'

'Correct.' Akhil Banerjee stroked his chin, 'And after Mr Agarwal showed us the ring. . . .'

'Mr Agarwal left the room once too, didn't he?' interrupted Chandan Mukherjee. 'I mean, not counting the time he went to get the ring. I think he must have gone to use the washroom.'

'Yes, Chandan babu. You are right,' agreed Akhil Banerjee. 'And after he showed us the ring. . . .'

'Sujit Hazra left almost immediately,' offered Bibhuti Bose. 'He tripped and fell, and stooped down to collect his things. I remember helping him, as I was the closest.'

'I bet he fell on purpose. Just to distract the rest of us,' offered Chandan Mukherjee. 'In that commotion he must have quietly slipped the ring into his pocket.'

'Criminals, criminals!' said Bibhuti Bose.

'But how did Sujit have time to. . . .'

'Arrey, Joj Saheb, don't you know these thieves? Their hands work so fast. He distracted us very cleverly with his fall, and managed to pocket the ring when no one was looking. Byas!' said Chandan Mukherjee throwing his hands up in the air.

Debdas Guha Roy looked at his watch. 'I have to go.' He got up. 'I have a class this morning.'

The others got up too. *'Cholee,'* (I'm leaving), they said to each other as was the custom.

Bibhuti Bose and Chandan Mukherjee made their way to the paan and cigarettes stall at the corner of the park. Akhil Banerjee was already a few paces ahead, when Debdas Guha Roy caught up with him.

'Joj Saheb?' he coughed. 'I was saying,. . . .?'

'Yes, Debdas babu?'

'Do you think it was Sujit Hazra too?'

'Huh? Well I don't know . . . I have to think about it.'

'Have you formed any other idea? Do you mind telling me?'

'Perhaps you have formed an idea yourself, Debdas babu?' smiled Akhil Banerjee.

'It is not that, Joj Saheb,' Debdas Guha Roy hesitated, making sure no one was within earshot. 'You see, yesterday at the meeting, when Mr Agarwal said that thing about inviting us . . . did you notice the way he looked at me? I mean, it's nothing really . . . but. . . .'

'But what, Debdas babu?'

'I have an uneasy feeling he thinks . . . he thinks . . . that I have stolen his ring.' The words came out with much effort. He smiled sheepishly.

'You?!'

'Yes, well . . . maybe I am wrong, but you know given my background in geology . . . maybe he thinks that I will have some idea about the price . . . It is ridiculous really . . . why would I. . . .?'

'Relax, Debdas babu, no one suspects you. I have good instincts when it comes to sniffing out culprits. And you my friend are no thief, ha ha ha.' He patted Debdas Guha Roy good-humouredly on his back.

Debdas Guha Roy let out an imperceptible sigh of relief.

'It's so hot today, isn't it?' he said, intending to change the topic, and then remembered that the weather had already been dwelt upon. Akhil Banerjee might have sensed his awkwardness, for he mentioned an appointment, said a hasty goodbye and quickened his pace.

To Find A Suitable Boy

The morning's paper contained the following article.

Theft at Golf Garden prompts local youth to take action.

The theft of a very rare and expensive diamond ring, believed to have belonged to the Late Queen Ratna Kumari of Garhwal, has prompted the local youth of Golf Garden, Sabuj Kalyan Samiti to take matters of security into their own hands.

'We cannot just sit back and watch our neighbourhood being looted,' said Partho Roy, who will be leading the other young men of his locality in keeping night-time vigil.

What is perhaps most shocking is that this theft took place in full view of several people, most notable among them being Retd. High Court Judge Akhil Banerjee, who resides in Mr Agarwal's neighbourhood. The disappearance was noticed almost immediately after the guests had left. The police are still on the look-out for a Sujit Hazra, who earlier came to Mr Agarwal's house on the pretext of selling curio items. He has been described as a lean man in his thirties, with black wavy hair, a beard and a moustache.

Subhojit Kanti, local MLA and member of the opposition party has called the law and order situation of the state 'deplorable'. In light of the present incident, he has urged more young men to follow the example of Partho Roy, indicating that it is time for the mantle of responsibility to shift from the hands of a passive and unresponsive government.

★

'Korta babu, someone is here to see you,' Kanai handed Akhil Banerjee a visiting card.

Akhil Banerjee glanced at it. 'Seat him in the living room. I will be down in two minutes.'

As Akhil Banerjee entered the room, Mr Agarwal stood up, hands folded in *namaskar*, a congenial smile pasted over his round face.

'I have come to apologize, sir,' he hastened before Akhil Banerjee could open his mouth. 'Yesterday at the Club house, my manner was most impolite. I did not mean to insinuate my guests, sir. Please accept my apologies.'

'It's alright, Mr Agarwal. Please take a seat.'

'The last few weeks have been very. . . .' Mr Agarwal trailed off. 'The thing is . . . this ring was an extremely valuable item for me. It belonged to my late wife you see. . . .'

'I'm really sorry for your loss, Mr Agarwal.'

'I have so many valuable things in my house you know, Judge Saab. Now the police have come and seen everything. Who is to say that they will not appoint some goons to loot my place? Times are so bad . . . one doesn't know whom to trust,' he sighed.

Kanai appeared with two glasses of fresh lime juice.

'Mr Agarwal, do you suspect someone yourself?' asked Akhil Banerjee .

'Thank you, sir,' said Mr Agarwal, accepting the glass offered. 'Well . . . the servants have all been with me for ages. Initially, I did think it was one of them. But then . . . they have had ample opportunity all these years . . . Besides, for any of them to take the ring, he would have to be alone in the room. And I tell you, I never once left the room. The police took them away for questioning and found nothing.'

'After you showed us the ring, you left the box on the bookshelf in the living room, didn't you?'

'Well, yes. I got up to put it back in the safe in my bedroom, but then we started talking about Jamini Roy, remember? So I just put it on the bookshelf for the time being.'

'You didn't happen to check the box at the time?'

'Well, no. I mean, why should I? I assumed that the ring was still there, and I simply put the box on the bookshelf.'

'Hmm . . . and after we left . . . .?'

'I sat down on the easy chair with a magazine. After about half an hour or so, I felt tired and wanted to retire to bed. I took the box from the shelf . . . I don't know what made me check this time. I opened it and it was empty! I notified the police immediately.'

'Who else lives in your house?'

'Apart from my servants, there is Bikash Bakshi, my personal secretary. You met him that day. He has been with me for five years now. He left immediately after showing all the guests in. Sunday is usually his day off.'

'Hmm . . . At the moment, all fingers seem to be pointing at Sujit Hazra. If only there was a way to track him down.'

'It must have been him. I'm sure of it. Unfortunately, I have no idea where he lives or works. The ring is gone,' sighed Mr Agarwal.

Akhil Banerjee's brows were knitted in concentration. 'Mr Agarwal,' he said presently, 'would it be possible to see your living room once more?'

'Why yes, of course. It would be my pleasure. When would you like to drop by?'

'Shall we say 5 o'clock this evening?'

★

Chhaya Guha Roy tossed away the Bengali paper nonchalantly. A close scrutiny of the matrimonial columns revealed, to her utter disappointment, that not too many suitors were in the market these days. Ever since Piya, her elder daughter had finished her M.A. in English, the thought of finding a suitable groom, was uppermost in Chhaya Guha Roy's mind. It was useless to bring it up with her husband, who would much rather disappear under the newspaper, or turn on the television. Really, his insouciance on a matter as important as this was disconcerting. On rare occasions when she broached the subject making sure that neither paper nor television was going to be a distraction, Debdas Guha Roy's response was predictable. Have you spoken to Piya about it? He would ask. She's only twenty-three. May be she wants to study a bit more, or look for a job.

Chhaya Guha Roy was a reasonable lady. She had nothing against Piya continuing with her education, or starting a career. But she failed to see how any of that could be an excuse to postpone the search for a groom? After all, a girl had to get married and start a family *sometime.* If you asked Piya, she would naturally say she's not ready yet. The point is nobody is ever ready. One just has to do it, that's all!

When it had been time for Chhaya to get married (when she had barely turned twenty), she had agreed to the match without so much as asking for the boy's name. The choice of her parents and that of her grandmother and various other relations had been good enough for her. Come to think of it, she couldn't even remember being asked if she had any objections to the match. At least she had had the luxury of seeing her husband-to-be in person—albeit for fifteen minutes, in a room full of elders accompanied by noisy children, with inquisitive neighbours peeping through the windows of their ground floor flat in Gorcha Road.

The bottom line was that if she, Chhaya Guha Roy, M.A. in Bengali, wanted to see her daughter married and settled, then she, Chhaya Guha Roy, M.A. in Bengali, would have to do something about it. One just could not postpone things like this forever. After all who is to say, that even a good girl like Piya will not bring home a boyfriend (she winced at the thought) . . . someone from another caste? Or worse still, a 'non-Bengali'?

Though when she thought about it, she couldn't quite put a finger on what it was that was so objectionable about alliances from other states of India. After all, a kshatriya from Tamil Nadu or Uttar Pradesh was still a kshatriya, wasn't he? She thought of the term 'non-Bengali'. What was it about Bengalis that they liked to alienate themselves so? Did one ever hear of a 'non-Punjabi' or a 'non-Marathi'? No.

She wondered what it would be like to live in Tamil Nadu, and be constantly referred to as a 'non-Tamil' by the locals. It would be humiliating, she decided. Yet the word, 'non-Bengali' was never used in a humiliating or an offensive sense. It was a mere differentiation. Bengalis and non-Bengalis. Locals and foreigners. Us and them.

She forced herself to come out of her reflections, scrutinized the *Sunday Daily* in greater detail. There was always a possibility that she had overlooked an advertisement that would have suited Piya (and herself) quite well. Chhaya Guha Roy was now a veteran in deciphering messages hidden behind cryptic matrimonial bio-data. *Uh ma pa uh shya* meant '*Uchya Madhyamik* Passed, *Ujwal Shyambarna*'. In other words, the prospective groom had passed his Higher Secondary exams, and was of wheatish complexion, which was a polite way of saying 'not too dark'. It appalled Chhaya Guha Roy how some boys, with a mere 'pass' High School certificate from some C-grade institution, and with little or no career prospects whatsoever, dared to invite alliances from 'tall, fair, slim, beautiful girls with at least a college degree'. Moreover the girl needs to be adept in cooking, sewing, embroidery and various household chores. No one, it seemed, not one person in this country, no matter how intellectually challenged or financially unsound, wanted a bride who was anything short of Miss India endowed with the talents of Lata Mangeshkar. In all these months of groom-hunting Chhaya Guha Roy had not come across one matrimonial advertisement for a healthy, average-looking girl of medium to dark complexion. If only she had a son . . . the advertisement for her daughter-in-law would read 'Well-qualified girl from a respectable Indian (preferably Bengali) family wanted.' That was all that really mattered.

Not that Chhaya Guha Roy had reasons to worry about Piya. She was quite pleasant to look at, and at 5'4' was taller than most Bengali girls. Her complexion though, was a bit of an issue. Piya, far from being fair, was somewhat on the darker side of 'wheatish'. Apart from that, Piya was an M.A. in English from Calcutta University. She had been educated in a reputed all girls' Convent School, and had received training in semi-classical music. In short, a girl any mother-in-law would be delighted to have. No, the problem lay in the fact that all the well-qualified boys from good families, earning six figure salaries, somehow had not been born of Bengali parents and if they were, they happened to belong to other castes.

She cast the paper away in disgust. Three months of scanning had presented very slim prospects. Something more drastic was required. She would have to insert her daughter's matrimonial advertisement in the papers. And not just in the Calcutta edition, in the national dailies too. That would ensure a wider reach, and would undoubtedly fetch better results. The brilliance of her plan brought about a smile on her lips. But every good plan had its obstacles. And the hurdle here was to convince her husband, Debdas Guha Roy and their daughter Piya.

With a renewed sense of purpose, Chhaya Guha Roy started penning down the advertisement for her daughter's match-making, with particular attention to the abbreviations.

A Clue

Kanai handed the cordless receiver to Akhil Banerjee.

'Hello?'

'Hello, Joj Saheb? I just remembered something.' Bibhuti Bose sounded excited.

'Yes, Bibhuti babu?'

'You remember when Sujit fell down, some of his things spilled out of his bag. I had bent down to pick them up. There was a paper, a receipt from a hotel . . . I have been trying to remember the name for sometime now . . . And it finally came to me . . . Shuruchi Cabin, Lake Market. May be that is where he is staying, what do you think, Joj Saheb?'

'Hmm. Maybe. At least it is obvious that he has been there once. In any case, I will be seeing Rakshit later today. I will definitely inform him. Good work, Bibhuti babu.'

'Thank you, Joj Saheb. This is so exciting, as if we are in the midst of a detective novel. Of course it is not anything new for you, but for me . . . heh heh . . . I mean. . . .'

'Yes, yes, I understand.'

'Anyway, see you tomorrow morning Joj Saheb.'

'Yes, goodbye.'

★

The Sabuj Kalyan Samiti club house had come alive at the prospect of yet another year's Durga Pujo.

Durga Pujo was the worship of the Divine Mother. Goddess Durga, fondly referred to by all Bengalis as 'Ma', spends the greater part of the year, high atop the Kailash mountains in the Himalayas. Here she stays with her husband, Lord Shiva, The Destroyer of the Universe, best known for his fiery temper and sprightly dance routines. Every year in the autumn months, Ma Durga brings her four children for a vacation to her mother's home, which is more or less spread out all across Bengal. These four or five days of the annual visit therefore, constitute the Durga Pujo, a festival of gigantic proportions, where the goddess and her children are venerated and worshipped by the devotees. The exact dates of her arrival are dictated by the sacramental *Ponjika* – a sort of divine timetable – released each year after the cosmic charts have been studied carefully, and their various implications put down in a more readable format for the benefit of the ignorant. The gods, undoubtedly, like variety. Hence, each year – according to the *Ponjika* – she comes on a different 'vehicle'; an elephant, a boat, or a palanquin.

Doubts about how she could have managed the arduous journey, all the way from the Himalayas to the plains of Bengal, on these modest modes of transport are never aired. It is just one of those godly things that we mortals would never fathom. Why, out of the 330 million gods in India, should the people of Bengal choose to worship with fervour Ma Durga, is a matter of speculation, and not one that is likely to provide a conclusive answer. The story goes that a long, long time ago, there lived a demon called Mahishasura. He was half-man and half bull. Having performed various austerities and penances, he received a boon from the gods. The boon proclaimed that Mahishasura could never be killed by any man. Powered by the boon of immortality, he started committing atrocities in the three worlds. Now the gods had to do something to stop him, yet care needed to be taken that the boon was not compromised in any way. They were gods, after all!

So they came together and created a goddess (the boon had prevented Mahishasura from being killed by any man) and empowered her with all their energies. Thus was born Durga, the ten-armed goddess, a weapon in each of her ten arms. She came riding a lion and killed Mahishasura, bringing an end to all evil. According to legend, years later, Lord Rama, when embarking on his epic journey to kill the demon-king Ravana had performed the worship of the Goddess Durga in the autumn months. Durga Pujo thus symbolizes the victory of good over evil, of truth over untruth, of courage over cowardice. And these undoubtedly are the values that the people of Bengal cherish above all.

For some in the Sabuj Kalyan club, Durga Pujo was not only a week-long effort to please the goddess, *it was the very reason for staying alive.* Preparations and planning typically started months earlier. Collecting funds, designing the clay idols, selecting a theme, the lighting, the *pandals*, the decoration, the food stalls, the music, the theatres . . . the tasks were unending.

The Durga Pujo this year was a particularly serious affair. Ever since the Asian Paints Sharod Samman Awards had been announced, Milonee Club, the biggest club in the Golf Garden area, continued to be the all round winner. Be it lighting, decoration or ambience, the efforts of all the other clubs seem embarrassingly tame and pallid when compared to Milonee. It would not have mattered so much really, except that Milonee club housed its Durga Pujo just a stone's throw away from Sabuj Kalyan Samiti's. When devotees went *pandal*-hopping all night and day, they would cross Milonee first before reaching Sabuj Kalyan. The comparison then, was a little too stark. Unsuspecting passers-by, without so much as batting an eyelid, would pass flippant comments like 'So-so, nothing like Milonee club'. And in a matter of seconds, months of hardship would be reduced to dust.

The rivalry had now reached personal levels. Sudhir Bagchi, President of Milonee Club, at a recent gathering had amused the guests by taunting Biplab Maity, President of Sabuj Kalyan Samiti. He called Sabuj Kalyan's attempts 'amateurish' at best.

'Why do you go through all the trouble of collecting *chanda*, and calling meetings for this, Biplab?' he had asked. The 'paraphernalia' he had said was a 'wasted effort'. Even Sudhir Bagchi's five-year-old son had more creative ideas. The final insult had come when Sudhir Bagchi actually asked Biplab Maity, if he should ask his five-year-old son to give Sabuj Kalyan some ideas for the Pujo this year.

This year's meeting was being held almost three months before the Pujo. 'There is no time to lose,' Biplab Maity asserted. 'We have got to beat those ***.' Normally one would never hear Biplab Maity use such derogatory language, but the stress of yet another year's Durga Pujo, coupled with the daunting task of robbing Milonee of this year's award, was too much to handle.

Partho, Bappa, Pinaki, Jishu, Joy, Somen, Poltu and Bhombol were seated on the floor. Biplab hoisted himself on the desk, sending off a cloud of dust. The tension in the room was palpable.

'Ideas boys, ideas!' Attempts to infuse enthusiasm by thus raising his voice were replied with deep sighs. Bappa blew air out from the corner of his mouth. Bhombol shifted his weight purposefully from one side to the other. Jishu clapped his hands to kill a mosquito that had been buzzing around him. In the blank faces that stared back at him, Biplab Maity could almost read another year's humiliation.

'We need to raise more funds,' Bappa volunteered finally.

'How? And what do we do with those funds?'

'Lighting,' added Bhombol.

'Lighting?'

'Yes, Biplab da. All the top *pujos* in Calcutta are now a play of lighting. It is the lighting that will attract the devotees first. Right from Ghulam Mohammed Shah Road up to Sabuj Kalyan Park, on either side of the street we can have attractive *jhikimiki* lights. It will be like enticing the prey till they reach the point of no-return. The devotees will gape at these and before they know it, they will find themselves right in front of the *pandal* entrance.'

'We can do the collapse of the Twin Towers or the statue of Saddam falling off the pedestal. *Darun darun*!' said Jishu excitedly.

'Twin towers? Saddam? Who are we doing this Pujo for? Terrorists?!'

'*Bah!* Don't you remember the Pujo last year at Friends' Colony? They showed the train blast with lights? First the train was lit up, then passengers were shown getting in, and then came the sound of a loud explosion, and everything being blown to smithereens. Then everything goes dark, and the message "Be Alert!

Prevent Acts of Terrorism" was lit up. The show had attracted a huge crowd. I myself must have watched it a few hundred times,' said Bhombol.

'We can show the Katrina tragedy. Scores of houses getting washed away by the hurricane . . . The effects of the lighting would be spectacular, I tell you. We can move the audience to tears,' offered Somen.

'Katrina? Do you ever read news of any country other than America? This is the big problem with this country's youth, with your generation.' Biplab da clicked his tongue. The few years that lay between Biplab and the other boys of the Club, somehow translated to a 'generation' in Biplab's mind. 'You cannot think beyond the US of A.'

'We don't have to show Katrina. How about the Tsunami? Same lighting, same effect, yet very local.'

'Tsunami? What is this? A Pujo for the depressed? Do you think people come to *pandals* to be sad?' he grunted.

'My god! I've got it!' cried Bappa so loud, that Partho and Bhombol seated on either side of him almost leaped in the air.

'What now, Bappa? You have thought of another tragedy? The Hiroshima bombing perhaps? Pearl Harbour? Why not show the whole World War?'

'No, no Biplab da. This is a great idea, I tell you, great idea! See Ma Durga comes to earth each year to destroy all the evil right? The evil here is the demon, Mahishasura? Right? Right? So how if we this year, make the face of the demon like that of Osama Bin Laden? Huh?' Bappa looked about for the effect his words had created. It was as if his friends were spellbound and speechless.

Even Biplab da, who was staring at the floor, was too awestruck to move. 'Bappa, my boy,' he said eventually, 'You're an idiot.'

The Club house door creaked open. Bibhuti Bose and Chandan Mukherjee walked in.

'Arrey, Biplab, you are doing something here tonight? We are scheduled to have a bridge game here,' said Bibhuti Bose.

'Sorry kaku, the Club house will not be available tonight. We are having a meeting.'

'Meeting? About what? The security of this neighbourhood? I must tell you Partho, you and your boys make an awful lot of noise at night. All that banging of lathis and the shrill whistling . . . Quite unnecessary really. Please try to keep it down a bit.'

'Kaku, I'm surprised you can hear us at all! The way you snore (ha ha) is enough to keep the whole neighbourhood awake . . . what do you say Somen?' The boys chuckled.

'What is this "very important meeting" about, Biplab? If it is something concerning our community, then we need to know about it,' said Chandan Mukherjee.

'It is about this year's Pujo, kaku,' replied Biplab. 'We are thinking of starting early this year.'

'Pujo meeting? How come I did not get any notice? Did you Bibhuti babu?'

Bibhuti Bose shook his head.

'What, Biplab? This is a major overlook on your part. How come none of the seniors were informed? You must make sure that everyone is involved right from the start. After all, the Pujo is for everyone . . . not just for you or for me.'

'Kaku,' replied Biplab, getting off the desk, and straightening to his full height, 'this year we have decided to let the seniors rest. Pujo is a lot of hard work. It requires commitment, dedication. This year we have decided to organize the *pujo* ourselves.'

'What are you saying, Biplab?' Chandan Mukherjee sounded incredulous. 'No no, this won't do. Arrey, we have . . . *iye*, what do you call it . . . 'commitment' and 'dedication'. We can. . . .'

'Kaku,' Biplab raised his hand gesturing Chandan Mukherjee to stop. 'This is for the best. Trust me. We cannot afford to lose to Milonee Club every year. Our Pujo is outdated and predictable. We need fresh ideas, we need young blood. We. . . .'

Chandan Mukherjee opened his mouth to utter words of protest. Bibhuti Bose touched him lightly in the arm. 'Come on, moshai. Let the boys continue with their meeting,' he said. 'We have to inform the others that tonight's game is cancelled.' The two of them turned to leave.

'Don't forget to visit our *pandal*, kaku. You must come with your families,' called out Biplab.

★

Assistant Commissioner of Police, Sudarshan Rakshit, had a personality that befitted his name. At 5' 11', he was taller than the average Bengali man by at least half a foot. His chiselled face and keen eyes with the steel-framed spectacles, matched an attitude that said 'No nonsense, please.'

'So Joj Saheb, the night of 7th July . . . .'

'Yes, Rakshit, about that . . . I was wondering if you had made any progress.'

Sudarshan Rakshit smiled.

'Of course you don't have to tell me exactly what progress you have made, Rakshit. I respect your confidentiality concerns,' hastened Akhil Banerjee.

Sudarshan Rakshit offered a cup of tea to Akhil Banerjee, and took a sip from his own. 'Normally I would not discuss a case with anyone. But with you sir, it is slightly different. Not only are you a respected judge, but you were also present at the scene of the crime.'

'Retired judge,' corrected Akhil Banerjee.

'I have questioned the three servants,' continued Sudarshan Rakshit. 'Bahadur was at the gate the whole time. He swears that he did not leave even once. He had let in six people including Sujit Hazra. That leaves the other two. The cook was in the kitchen the whole time. I double checked that with Bablu, the manservant who was bringing in snacks and tea. Bablu was the only one with ample opportunity to steal it, amongst the domestic help. He had come in several times and could have taken the ring. But,' he shook his head, 'with all of you right there. . . .'

'Hmm . . . I agree.'

'And Mr Agarwal swears he did not leave the room after all of you left . . . I am afraid it only means that it would have to be one of the guests.'

'Yes, I see that,' nodded Akhil Banerjee. 'I suppose you have interrogated everyone?'

'Everyone, except Sujit Hazra. Mr Agarwal could not provide any hints to his whereabouts.'

'I have information for you, Rakshit' said Akhil Banerjee and he recounted his earlier conversation with Bibhuti Bose.

'Hmm, this is a definite lead,' nodded Sudarshan Rakshit as he jotted down the name.

'Though, Rakshit. . . .' hesitated Akhil Banerjee.

'Sir?'

'Bibhuti babu . . . well, as eager as he is to help, I'm afraid one can't rely too much on his memory of names. It might as well be Shujata, Shyamali, Shuchi . . . you never really know.'

'Oh, I see what you mean. I will see what I can do. Banerjee?' He called out to his colleague. 'See if you can find a Shuruchi, Shujata, Shuchi Cabin in the Lake Market, Lake Road area.'

'Well anyway,' he continued, turning to Akhil Banerjee, 'It seems Sujit had called about a week or so before the party, asking for an appointment. Mr Agarwal had never met him before. He was a complete stranger to everyone. And he left much before the others (I presume with the ring). He had a beard and moustache, could have easily been a disguise. You know these crooks, sir . . . they gain entry into a gentleman's house on some pretext, and the next thing you know, you have been robbed of everything. Imagine how daring he must have been. To have stolen, right in front of a judge . . . '

'Yes, that is exactly what I was wondering,' said Akhil Banerjee. He finished his tea and got up.

'Rakshit, thank you for your time.'

'Arrey, sir, it's my pleasure. I will keep you posted of any development.'

'Good day to you.'

'Okay, sir.'

★

'Mr Agarwal, if you don't mind, may I ask you a question?' Akhil Banerjee and Mr Agarwal were seated in the familiar living room. Tea and biscuits had been served.

'Of course, Juj Saab. Anything.'

'You had moved into this neighbourhood almost five years ago, am I right?'

Mr Agarwal nodded.

'And in these five years you have not made any attempts to know your neighbours. You have always preferred to keep to yourself. Correct? Then why did you suddenly. . . .'

'Yes, yes, I see what you mean, Juj Saab. It is true I have been very unsocial. In fact, I avoid human company as much as possible. But for the last few months, I have been feeling very . . . very lonely, Juj Saab. You may not be able to understand it. You are a very lucky man . . . you have a family, children, grandchildren. But I have nobody in this world I can call my own, nobody.' Mr Agarwal's voice became throaty.

'My wife died five years ago. I have never quite recovered from the shock. I like to keep to myself. Read books, look at my collections. But once in a while I miss company, company of learned, interesting people such as yourself. So when I read in the papers that our revered Judge Akhil Banerjee has retired, I thought why not call Juj Saab to my house now that he has more time. We can get to know each other better. And I thought of inviting a few other elderly gentlemen from this neighbourhood too, that's all.'

Akhil Banerjee nodded. He finished his cup of tea and got up to leave. But instead of going towards the exit door, he walked towards the bookshelf. The velvet box was not there.

'Did the police take the box for evidence?'

'You mean fingerprints? They did, but I had passed the box around to everyone remember? All your prints are there.'

'All our prints, you mean. You held the box, too,' smiled Akhil Banerjee.

'Yes, yes, of course!'

Akhil Banerjee stared at the bookshelf, and then turned slowly around. He pictured the scene from the party a week ago. They had all been right there, looking at the ring, passing it around. Then Sujit Hazra got up to leave . . . And in an instant he knew what had happened.

It was the why that now bothered him.

A Secret Club (For Senior Citizens Only)

Chhaya Guha Roy took out a neatly-pressed blue silk sari and weighed it against the parrot green that had been placed on the bed earlier. She contemplated a moment or two. The parrot green sari certainly looked more expensive, but it had the distinct disadvantage of making a 'wheatish' complexion appear much darker than it actually was. A folly of this nature could prove to be fatal. She thrust aside the parrot green sari and took out a red one. Too gorgeous, almost fit for bridal wear . . . one shouldn't be too presumptuous here. Off-white chiffon? Too much of an old maid's colour.

'I'm saying, is Piya home yet?' Debdas Guha Roy's anxious voice interrupted the selection process.

'No, she said she would return by four today,' answered Chhaya Guha Roy. 'Dutta babu said they would be here at five-thirty.'

'Are you sure? Oh, okay I see. Umm, what do I need to bring from the market? Samosas, sweets?'

'No no! I am making samosas at home. You bring the roshogollas, and the six rupee sweet . . . Ice cream sandesh they call it.'

'Six rupees per piece? How many do I have to bring? For five people, six rupees per piece and two sweets per head, amounts to sixty rupees on sandesh alone. Plus the cost of roshogollas, samosas, and the cashew nuts you are planning to serve. And we are not even going to see the boy today. If such meetings become frequent I will be bankrupt before the wedding day arrives.'

'What ominous things are you saying? Why should there be so many meetings? You don't think they will like our Piya? She is one in a thousand . . . any family would be delighted to bring her home . . . she is well-mannered and cultured, has a good singing voice. . . .'

Debdas Guha Roy slipped out of the house quietly as his wife continued to list her daughter's many fine qualities.

Piya arrived shortly after five, and rolled her eyes in response to her mother's menacing glare. Chhaya Guha Roy did not want to launch a verbal attack. There was too much to do, and ruining Piya's mood was not going to help.

The next half hour was a test of patience for mother and daughter.

'Why do I need to wear a sari?' demanded Piya, as she struggled with the pleats that clearly looked like they should have been someplace else. Her mother attended to the sari, as she instructed Diya to do her sister's hair.

'There is no time, there is no time,' she muttered for the hundredth time.

'What are you going to do? Ask Baba to do my make-up now?'

'Quiet, Piya! Don't talk like that. In fact, don't talk at all in front of them. Just politely answer whatever they ask you. And remember to smile always. Now apply some powder on your face. It's looking so dark and pale. How many times have I asked you to take an umbrella when going out in the sun?

'Arrey, you listening?' she called out to her husband. 'Go and stand on the main road . . . maybe they are not being able to locate the house. It is so confusing the way they have numbered houses on this street.'

'Hurry, hurry! Put some kajal or mascara or whatever it is that girls put on their eyes these days. And sit on that chair next to the bookshelf. The lighting there would be just perfect . . . that must be the sound of their taxi. Hurry, hurry,' Chhaya Guha Roy rushed out of the room.

'Sit on that chair next to the bookshelf. The lighting there would be just perfect,' mimicked Piya. 'And at only five rupees a head, you can now watch today's theatre *Piya raani se shaadi karega kaun*?'(Who will marry Queen Piya?)

'Sssh, didi,' whispered Diya. 'They are here.'

★

The Duttas were in all four people. Mr and Mrs Dutta (the boy's parents) and another elderly couple introduced to the Guha Roys as the boy's paternal uncle and aunt. Mrs Dutta, who had approached the solitary chair by the bookshelf, had been skilfully guided to another 'more comfortable' seat. Sweets and savouries had been served and the conversation hovered over the day's weather and how difficult it was to find addresses in Calcutta these days. Presently Diya was asked to go see if her sister was ready.

Piya entered with a tray of samosas in her hand. Chhaya Guha Roy hastened to help her daughter and indicated to her to go touch the feet of the guests.

'It's not necessary at all,' offered Mrs Dutta even as she put out her feet to facilitate the gesture of respect. Piya hesitated, glanced at her mother, whose glare clearly indicated that a social solecism of this nature would not be permitted. She obliged, and seated herself on the chair by the bookshelf.

'So how far have you studied?' asked Mrs Dutta sweetly.

'I have an M.A. in English Literature.'

'Very good, very good.'

'What do you plan to do after this? Study some more or take up a job?' It was the boy's uncle questioning now. 'Of course these days there are not too many opportunities for an Arts graduate. Why did you not pursue the sciences?'

Piya, who could think of several good reasons, simply decided to say, 'I have a job.'

'Oh you do? Very good . . . where do you work?'

'I give private tuitions to high school and college students.'

'Oh I see. Private tutor,' the disappointment was apparent. 'How much does one earn in private tuitions? 1500, 2000 rupees a month? That is not really a career. You know there is a saying, heh heh "Those who can: do. Those who can't: teach" . . . heh heh heh.' He chuckled.

Piya looked at her father, who was staring hard at the floor. She stood up from her seat and looked at the boy's uncle. 'I'm afraid we don't find your joke funny, Mr Dutta. My father is a retired professor. In this house we take teaching very seriously. In future, it would be advisable that you take some time to study the biodata accompanying the girl's photograph.'

And with those words she marched out of the room, leaving behind gaping mouths and raised eyebrows.

★

The day was hot and humid. The leaves of the gulmohar trees, brown and parched from the heat, stood still. Debdas Guha Roy seated himself on the bench and watched a yellow lizard dart about on the tree trunk. Akhil Banerjee was already doing his daily rounds, but the others had not arrived yet.

Debdas Guha Roy glanced at his watch, 5:30. He was earlier than usual, but then, he hadn't really slept the night before. Uneasy, discomforting thoughts had raced through his mind all night long. What if he was unable to find a good home for Piya? Piya is a wonderful child. A bit short-tempered perhaps, but definitely one any family would be delighted to bring home. But then, how does one find a good home? One reads of so many things in the papers these days, stories of how young brides have been tortured for dowry or mistreated for any number of reasons. What if Piya ends up in one such home? It was so difficult to recognize the goodness in people these days. Back in his childhood, things were different. One could always tell a good man from a bad one. Every man's soul is reflected in his eyes, his father would say. He could take one look at someone, and tell with certainty whether the man could be trusted or not. These days things were not so simple. Appearances were deceptive. People were cunning, crafty. Situations and events, you could never conceive of even ten years ago, were becoming increasingly rampant. How could. . . .

'What are you pondering on this early in the day?'

Debdas Guha Roy looked up to find a smiling Chandan Mukherjee approaching the bench, swinging a walking stick by his side.

'Oh, good morning Chandan babu,' replied Debdas Guha Roy. 'Didn't see you coming.'

'Something serious?,' asked Chandan Mukherjee, as soon as he was seated.

'*Arrey* no no . . . just like that . . . others seem to be late today? Should I order tea?'

'Let's wait till Joj Saheb finishes his walk.'

The two of them sat in silence for a while. Some of the neighbourhood boys were playing football. A deflated leather ball was being kicked around with bare feet in all directions. A quarrel had ensued between the two rival teams over a free-kick.

'*Arrey* Saar? Are you well?' A robust looking man called out to Debdas Guha Roy from across the park. Debdas Guha Roy raised his right hand in response.

'Who is that, moshai?' asked Chandan Mukherjee.

'Khokon. Lives in Haripada Das Lane. Used to be my student. Do you know what he does now?'

'What?'

'He is a script-writer.'

'Script-writer? For what?'

'*Arrey*, all these Bengali films and TV serials. Haven't you noticed how many exclusive Bengali channels are there on cable these days? I hear Khokon has been doing well.'

This fact became evident as Khokon walked towards the foursome. Several chains of various metals clanked around his neck, and the rings on his stubby fingers shone with red, green and white stones. He stooped down to touch 'Saar's' feet.

'How are you doing, saar?'

'Getting along. What are you writing these days Khokon?'

'Saar, producers are after my life. New stories, crimes, murders . . . tell me how many of these can I come up with in a week? But this time I'm trying something very sensational.'

'Really? Tell us.'

Khokon's tone became serious in a theatrical way.

'Five people are murdered overnight. No violence, no bloodshed, no break-ins, nothing. Police are baffled.'

'Then how do these murders happen?'

'Anthrax.'

'Anthrax?'

'Yes, anthrax. You see, the villain sends ordinary letters to his victims, except that these letters are smeared with anthrax. One sniff . . . byaas, you are dead. What do you think, Saar?'

Debdas Guha Roy cleared his throat. 'Very good, Khokon. Ah . . . who is the hero?'

'Raghab da, saar. Our Raghab Chatterjee. Top hero these days, Saar. Lives in the top floor of Ahabaan Apartments, right there,' he pointed to some high-rises in the distance.

'Nice, nice. Good to see you doing so well, Khokon.'

'I have to run, Saar. We are shooting in Nalban today. I will tell you more of my stories another time. *Cholee*,' he said hastily and left.

'Ah! Here comes Bibhuti babu . . . Good morning sir! You are late today,' called out Chandan Mukherjee.

Bibhuti Bose, greeted everyone, and took his place in the bench, between Debdas Guha Roy and Chandan Mukherjee. Akhil Banerjee joined them presently, continuing with his free-hand exercises near the bench.

'Bibhuti babu, who is your bridge partner now? I hear Jyoti da is not coming to the Club these days?' asked Debdas Guha Roy.

'*Arrey* moshai, we cannot play at the Club anymore,' answered Bibhuti Bose.

'Why not?'

'These scoundrels, Partho and Biplab . . . they have their meetings there every day now. Who will fight with them, moshai? Have you heard the way they talk to us these days?'

'Bibhuti babu, you do not realize the reason for this sudden change of behaviour,' said Chandan Mukherjee. 'You see, a couple of years ago these fellows would not have dared to talk to us like this. Do you know why? It is because back then we were all gainfully employed. These boys, who think they can manage a Pujo without so much as informing us, these very same boys, used to come to our doorsteps like a bunch of sheep, asking for corporate advertisements. I have brought them thousands of rupees worth of advertisements. We all have. But now they know those days are gone. There is nothing more to be squeezed out of these oldies now. So why bother? Times have changed, Bibhuti babu. No use getting emotional about this,' he sighed and lit a Filter Will's cigarette.

Akhil Banerjee finished his exercises and wiped his glasses with a handkerchief.

'Chandan babu, are you saying that just because we have retired from our professional lives, we have to retire from everything else as well?' he asked. 'What is the point in living then? We still have 10, 15, 20 years to live. Are we going to spend the rest of our lives brooding just because these fellows don't give us due respect, or are we going to make use of this time to do all those things that we wanted to, but could not because of our demanding jobs?'

'What can we do now, Joj Sahib? At this age. . . .' started Bibhuti Bose.

'You see, this is the problem with our generation. We think activity is directly linked to earning capacity. And we try to justify the behaviour of all others by this one parameter . . . retirement. Some young fellows are rude to us, we think, oh it's only because we are retired. But the truth is harder to swallow. . . .'

'What do you mean, Joj Sahib?'

'We think others don't respect us, but in reality we don't respect ourselves.'

'Why do you say that, moshai? We have all had respectable jobs. You in particular Joj Saheb. you have held one of the most prestigious posts in the country.'

'Yes, yes, I agree with all that. I don't mean to say that we disrespect the jobs that we have done, or the life that we have led so far. Of course not! All I am saying is, once we retired, all that pride . . . that satisfaction somehow evaporated. That somehow, being unemployed has broken our spirits. Wouldn't you say? And it has nothing to do with money . . . we all have enough to live comfortably for the rest of our lives . . . but somehow somewhere there is a lack . . . as if we had more to give, but no one really wants or needs us anymore. Wouldn't you agree?'

Chandan Mukherjee nodded.

Bibhuti Bose's face turned serious. 'What more can I give, moshai? I have been giving all my life. . . .' he sighed heavily.

'Bibhuti babu, let me ask you . . . what do you do all day?'

Bibhuti Bose shrugged. 'I get up, have my tea, go to the market, have lunch, watch TV . . . so on and so forth. Nothing that important.'

'Exactly my point! Nothing important. Nothing substantial. Nothing that would add any value to anybody's life. Not to mine, not to yours, not to the person next door. Why is this, *hyan*? Who says that when so and so retires, he shall lead a life that is filled with boredom, predictability and everyday mundane things? Why is that? Why can't we do something useful? Something exciting? Something that makes us feel good about ourselves?'

'What can we do Joj Sahib, at this age? . . .' mumbled Chandan Mukherjee.

'Again the age! I am not asking you to climb Mount Everest, am I?'

'Yes, but still. . . .'

'I am with you, Joj Saheb,' announced Debdas Guha Roy suddenly. 'What do you propose we do?'

'Well, we could do some social work? May be start a school for these urchins who waste their time playing in the sun all day?' He pointed to a couple of half-naked children who were racing bicycle tyres, egging them on with sticks.

'You are right, Joj Saheb,' said Debdas Guha Roy. 'The *iye* we used to have as young men . . . where did that disappear? We let everyone walk all over us these days! These boys insult us, we digest it! The taxi-wallahs, rickshaw-wallahs, auto-wallahs insult us, we digest it!'

'The vegetable vendors give us rotten vegetables, we digest it!' quipped Bibhuti Bose.

'We think, what is the point in fighting with them? We are old now, our time has gone,' continued Chandan Mukherjee.

'We digest, we digest, and we digest! And then one day, we are dead! What a life!' said Debdas Guha Roy.

'True, true,' continued Bibhuti Bose. 'But Joj Sahib, do you propose we pick up a fight with those boys in the club house? They will just laugh and say something insulting again.'

'No, no, Bibhuti babu,' said Akhil Banerjee. 'I am not suggesting anything of the sort. We will not have to go to them. Sooner or later, they will come back to us. Just wait and see . . . Let us forget about Biplab and his gang for the time being. We have a more serious matter to concentrate on.' He paused to make sure that he had everyone's attention.

'The other day at Mr Agarwal's house, something quite serious happened. A very valuable item went missing, and we may have been the only witnesses. I want to do some investigation on my own, but I was wondering if you gentlemen would like to help too.'

'A private investigator? Arribbaas!' Debdas Guha Roy clapped his hands in glee. He could stay seated no longer. 'What do we have to do?'

'I'll tell you. But first, who is with me?'

'I am, sir,' replied Debdas Guha Roy, almost clicking his heels.

Bibhuti Bose and Chandan Mukherjee exchanged glances.

'*Iye*,' began Chandan Mukherjee. 'I'm not so sure. I have never done anything like this. It might be a bit *iye* for my age. . . .'

'*Iye*?'

'You know, risky . . . doesn't it seem like a boyhood fantasy? I mean we have all read Sherlock Holmes and Poirot, and our very own Bomkesh Bokshi and Feluda . . . and I am sure there is hardly a boy who hasn't fantasized about being a detective in his childhood . . . but don't you think we are a little too old to indulge in these fantasies now?'

'Being a detective in real life can be a lot less glamorous that these books make them out to be, Chandan babu. I can assure you, you will not be required to chase a culprit up the wall, or punch anyone in the face. Besides, I have formed a certain theory regarding what happened the other night . . . but there are some loose ends. I just would like to see if we can arrive at the truth. That's all. I could do it by myself, of course. I just thought it would be more fun for all of us to be in it together.'

'Umm . . . I don't know, Joj Saheb,' mumbled Chandan Mukherjee.

'Very well, then. It's your decision. What about you, Bibhuti babu?'

'No no Joj Saheb. . . .' interrupted Chandan Mukherjee. 'I didn't mean that I won't join you . . . it's just that. . . .'

'I am in,' offered Bibhuti Bose. 'Arrey, Chandan babu, how many more years are we going to live? Let us have some fun . . . what do you say?' He gave his friend a pat on his back.

'Okay, I'm in,' said Chandan Mukherjee finally. 'Count me in, sir'.

'Very well. Here's what I'd like you to do. When you go home today, think about the events that took place that evening. May be some of us saw something but it did not appear to be significant in any way? So just think about the events. Also, one of us will have to speak to Dr Mullick. I don't really know him that well.'

'I can do it,' volunteered Bibhuti Bose. 'Anyway, I will have to see him about this constipation.'

Akhil Banerjee nodded. 'But here's the thing. Let this be strictly between us. No one should get an inkling that we are carrying on some investigations on our own. So don't mention this to anyone, not even your own families. Let us act normal, casual. We will meet here again tomorrow to discuss. Agreed?'

'Agreed. Agreed.'

'I feel alive already, moshai,' said Debdas Guha Roy, stretching his arms and doing a couple of sideward twists. Aloud he said, 'From this day forth we shall LIVE, not merely exist. Starting from today, right NOW. Let us feel alive again. Let us. . . . '

'What about a name?' interrupted Bibhuti Bose.

'What name?'

'*Bah!* We just formed our own detective club, and we won't have a name for it?' said Bibhuti Bose.

'I know, I know. How about The Sensational Seniors?' offered Chandan Mukherjee in a theatrical way.

'*Durr* moshai, is that a name?'

They got up and started to walk towards their homes.

'Okay then, how about Seniors Against Crime?'

Bibhuti Bose shook his head.

'Seniors for a Change?' volunteered Debdas Guha Roy.

Chandan Mukherjee clicked his tongue. 'Doesn't have the *iye*, moshai.'

A New Suspect

Sujit came out of the bathroom, droplets of water dripping down his neck, a chequered towel tied around his waist. His one-room apartment on the terrace of Amma's hotel in Lake Market was barely 100 square feet in area. The corrugated metal roof would turn his room into a furnace in the summer months, but at least he had his own bathroom.

The tiny room was sparsely furnished with a narrow bed, just wide enough to hold his lean frame, a table and a chair. Pegs attached behind the door held all the clothing he possessed. The walls were covered with calendars of previous years that had been retained for the pictures of the various deities they contained. It was in front of one such calendar that Sujit now circled a lit incense stick and muttered his prayers. His *puja* thus completed, he pushed the end of the incense stick into the hinges of the window frame. It was then that he saw them, and for a few seconds his heart froze.

A couple of policemen stood on the footpath opposite his apartment, glancing up and down the road, probably searching for an address. Sujit watched the men from behind the curtain as they walked up to a couple of people and asked questions. Then they walked up to Shucheta Cabin at the end of the road.

Sujit waited anxiously. Menacing thoughts raced through his mind. After what seemed like ages, the policemen came out, got into their van and drove away. Sujit heaved a deep sigh of relief. He looked at the tuft of hair that lay on the table. The disguise had been a clever idea, he thought to himself. But he would have to get rid of it now.

★

'Are you exercising, Mr Bose?' asked Dr Subodh Mullick as Bibhuti Bose lay down on the patients' bed.

'Yes, I walk everyday.'

Dr Subodh Mullick attached the sphygmomanometer on Bibhuti Bose's right arm, and told him to relax.

'Really?' asked Dr Subodh Mullick. 'I always see you sitting on the bench. You must walk a little, Mr Bose. Some physical activity is very important. If your body is not sufficiently tired, how will you sleep well at night, huh? You see how many sleeping pills you take? This is not good, not good at all.'

'Sleep does not come to me easily, Doctor babu.'

'How can it? Moderate exercise is required every day. No need to walk too fast, but not too slow either. So walk a little everyday . . . yes?'

Dr Mullick pressed the stethoscope in his ears and pressed the pump.

'140 by 100', he announced. 'A little high but not too bad. Now about the constipation. . . .'

Bibhuti Bose got off the bed and seated himself on the chair opposite Dr Mullick.

'One spoonful mixed in lukewarm water, outside of meals. Okay?' said the doctor as he scribbled on his prescription pad.

'Thank you, doctor babu.' Bibhuti Bose pushed a hundred rupee note across to the doctor and stood up. 'Oh by the way, did the police come to see you, about the Agarwal case?'

'Yes they did. But it's an open-and-shut case.'

'Really? You mean. . . .'

'It has to be one of the servants. Mr Agarwal should have been more cautious. You cannot have a house full of valuables and not expect them to steal anything.'

'Hmm . . . may be you are right,' thought Bibhuti Bose. 'The police questioned me thoroughly too. How many times did everyone get up? Who was doing what? Is it possible to remember everything, moshai?'

'By the grace of god, I have a phenomenal memory, Mr Bose,' boasted Dr Mullick as he reclined on his chair. 'I got up to use the washroom once. Mr Mukherjee went out for a smoke (how many times have I asked him to quit. Joj Saheb got up once to see the Jamini Roy painting. Mr Guha Roy went up to see the ring once more and Mr Agarwal left the room twice, once to get the ring and once to use the washroom. See I remember everything.'

'I see. And how many times did the servants come in?'

'Three – once to serve us tea and samosas, once to fill the trays with cashew nuts, and once to remove the empty cups. The last entry was just after the ring was shown. Sujit Hazra had left by then.'

'What about him, doctor babu? You don't think it is possible that he could have stolen the ring?'

'Hmm, it is always possible. But his only opportunity was when he was about to leave. He was sitting right next to you, he got up to leave but then he tripped and fell. And quickly collected his things and left in a hurry. Surely we would have seen something.'

'Bravo, doctor babu! Really phenomenal memory, moshai. Anyway, thank you for the check-up. Good night.'

'Good night, Mr Bose.'

★

Biplab, sat cross-legged on the floor of the Sabuj Kalyan Samiti club house, and stared at the piece of white paper in front of him. It contained four bullet points, which Biplab now regarded one by one.

Lighting

Pandal

Ambiance

Idol

Regarding lighting he would have to go to Chandannagar himself. Though they specialized in Vishwakarma Pujo, and this was somewhat of an off-season for them, still no harm checking it out. But the real issue of course was what to show by way of this lighting. He pondered over the various suggestions that had come up in the past meetings . . . Katrina, Tsunami, 9/11 tragedy . . . and sighed.

Pandal: The temple for Ma Durga and her four children – their home for the five days of the Pujo. It would have to be simply grand – with chandeliers, and marble statues and fountains. A miniature palace . . . yes that's it! A Palace! Ma Durga would be dressed like a Queen, and Lakshmi, Saraswati, Kartik and Ganesh would be the princesses and the princes. He started jotting down the thoughts that raced through his mind.

And the palace gardens (decorated with fountains and marble statues) will have swans and peacocks playing in them. Swans and peacocks!!!! He put four exclamation marks beside this point. Swan was the vehicle of Goddess Saraswati and peacock that of Lord Kartik. Subtle symbolism. His heart pounded with excitement. If only he could get the other animals belonging to Ganesh, Ma Durga and Lakshmi. The mouse was not a problem; plenty would be available in the local drainage system. Regarding the owl, he would have to check the bird sellers in New Market and Hatibagan. The big problem was the lion . . . how majestic it would be to have a lion in the *pandal.* The children would be so excited, and would want to visit over and over again. He might have a word with Photik, his old friend who works in the Gemini Circus. Now that the animals are not allowed to perform in the circus anymore, maybe he could negotiate with them.

His thought went on to the publicity banners.

Come meet Ma Durga and her children . . . they come to Sabuj Kalyan riding on live animals!!

His hands scribbled excitedly. The more he thought about it, the more he seemed to like the idea – innovative, daring and capable of pulling crowds to the *pandal.* He knew that one major criterion for the judges would be the potential for pulling crowds. For this very reason, the height of the pandal's entrance would have to be very low. If the entrance were too high, then one could easily catch a glimpse of the goddess from the streets. People would not even bother to get off their cars (finding a parking spot was a big problem during those days). All they would have to do was to crane their necks a little . . . and voila!

Some *pandals* had just a roof and were open from all sides, so that devotees could enter and leave from any side. What was the fun in having such a *pandal*? What about the long queues, the pushing, the anticipation? No, decided Biplab, only one entrance in the front and a very low one at that, so that people would be forced to park their cars at least a kilometre away, and come limping (from the discomfort of their newly purchased shoes coupled with countless hours of pandal hopping). As the thoughts raced through his mind, he found himself drawing a rough sketch for the pandal this year. There could be a pillar here, some flower pots there, perhaps a marble statue or two in the corner. . .

Devotees would wander in enjoying the beautiful fountains, the swans and the peacocks on the way. And the moment they come inside, they come face to face with a full-sized live lion! The shock element! Brilliant! And then. . . .

Biplab's reverie was interrupted by Somen and Bappa's giggling outside the Club House. The two of them were talking loudly, in the most uncouth, callous manner. What would Biplab do with these good-for-nothings, always chuckling at the most crass jokes, their voices always a few decibels higher than necessary, and their every utterance accompanied by an unnecessary jerking of shoulders and limbs? No wonder their Pujo was so inferior, so. . . .

The boys entered, and seeing Biplab da in the Club house, checked their chuckle. Biplab continued to scribble, pretending not to have heard them. One by one the boys filled the Club house, and sat down on the floor in a semicircle.

Eventually, Biplab stopped writing, and looked up.

'Friends, Bengalis, fellow Club Members,' he announced with great élan, 'Lend me your ears.'

★

Bibhuti Bose came out of the doctor's clinic, and took a deep breath. Too many thoughts crowded his mind. Something the doctor had said puzzled him. He started to walk back home, taking the longer route, walking past the new construction site of the CIT multi-storeyed buildings. There was a slight chill in the air. He walked alongside the pond, then past the slums where mostly the rickshaw-pullers dwelled. Smell of corn being burnt on fire reached his nostrils.

'How come you are home so early?' asked Joyoti Bose on answering the door. 'Did you quarrel with someone at the club again?'

'No no, we did not play bridge tonight. Biplab and his gang have their Pujo meetings there now.'

'Oh, I see,' Joyoti Bose returned to her favourite Bengali TV serial on the cable. Bibhuti Bose took off his slippers, washed his feet and changed into an informal night wear of chequered white and blue *lungi* and *fotua*. He plunged into his favourite sofa and chewed on the betel leaf. The title music of the tele-serial floated across to the living room. Bibhuti Bose got up to check whether Joyoti Bose was indeed engrossed in the television in the bedroom, then picked up his cordless receiver and dialled a number. The phone was answered after four rings.

'Hello, Chandan babu?'

'Ah, yes, Bibhuti babu?'

'Listen, I have to tell you something important.'

'Yes, Bibhuti babu, I'm listening. But please speak up, I can hardly hear you.'

'Remember the other day, when we were at the park, and Joj Sahib was asking us to recount what had happened at Mr Agarwal's house?'

'Yes.'

'Well, someone had lied. One of us.'

'What do you mean, Bibhuti babu?'

'Dr Mullick told me that he distinctly remembers that Debdas babu had walked up to the bookshelf to see the ring one more time before we left. And now that he tells me, I remember it too. It was just after Sujit Hazra had left. Mr Agarwal excused himself briefly. And then Debdas babu quietly got up and walked up to the bookshelf. Of course, I could not have seen what he was doing as my back was turned towards him.'

'Oh yes, I remember it too. But what are you suggesting, Bibhuti babu? That Debdas babu. . . .?'

'No, no I don't mean that he . . . Well, I am not sure . . . I mean why would he hide it from us?'

'Well, maybe he forgot, just like the rest of us?'

'It is always possible, but still. . . .'

'No, no, Bibhuti babu. I think you are exaggerating . . . it cannot be.'

'Hmm . . . perhaps you are right, Chandan babu. But consider this, if Debdas babu did get up to see the ring again as Dr Mullick said, then he is the last person to have seen it before the theft was discovered. That in itself makes him the prime suspect. But if the ring was stolen by Sujit already, then Debdas babu must have seen an empty box, is it not? In that case he should have raised an alarm right then. How come he did not say anything?'

'Hmm . . . I see what you mean.'

'Do you think we should tell Joj Saheb?'

'No, no, Bibhuti babu. It would be dangerous to jump to conclusions. We have known Debdas babu for years . . . I simply cannot believe that he could do such a thing. Has Dr Mullick mentioned this to the police?'

'He may have. But it has not occurred to him that Debdas babu could be . . . you know . . . he thinks one of the servants did it.'

'Hmm, I see. Well anyway I think we ought to keep this to ourselves.'

'Okay Chandan babu, as you say. Good night.'

'Good night.'

Mrs Bose

Debdas Guha Roy had just returned from the Allahabad Bank, Lake Gardens branch, when the phone rang. The caller, a Mrs Bose, was in town for only a few days, and had chanced upon a matrimonial advertisement in *The Statesman.* If it was not too terribly inconvenient, she would like to visit them that evening. Her son, the prospective groom, had engineering and MBA degrees from reputed institutes of the country, and was currently working in a multinational company in Mumbai.

Debdas Guha Roy liked the tone of her voice – soft, cultured, educated. He set up an appointment for 6 o' clock. Piya should be home by then, he thought. He found himself smiling as he replaced the receiver. He had a good feeling about this one. A very good feeling.

Chhaya Guha Roy, upon hearing the news, hurried off to the kitchen to set off the household machinery that preceded every important occasion. She emerged from the kitchen several times to hear the 'exact' conversation that had taken place between her husband and Mrs Bose.

'This is a much better alliance,' she said more than once. 'Those Duttas were all wrong for us, no manners, no etiquette. Even if they had approved of Piya, I would never have consented to the wedding.'

By late afternoon, the enthusiasm had mellowed down. 'They have only seen the advertisement in the newspaper. They haven't even seen the photo. At least the Duttas had approved of her photo,' pondered Chhaya Guha Roy as the smell of the fresh green peas stuffing wafted through the kitchen.

'So?' said Debdas Guha Roy. 'Piya is quite beautiful. She may not be all that fair, but she is not too dark either. She is qualified, well-mannered, homely . . . what else could the boy's family want?'

Any doubt that might have arisen regarding Piya's approvability was thus discarded.

★

Partho coughed politely.

'Yes, Partho?' asked Biplab.

'Biplab da, you have forgotten the fifth point. After pandal, lighting, etc. The most important point.'

'What is it?'

'Budget? Funds? How are we going to build a palace and have live animals for five days? Do you have any idea how much a lion will eat?'

'Hmm . . . budget . . . how much did we collect last year?'

'Six lakhs,' replied Jishu, the treasurer.

'Okay, so this year, simply double it. Twelve lakhs.'

'Twelve lakhs!!'

'Of course. How can we expect to beat Milonee with a meagre budget of six lakhs, tell me? They must be collecting at least fifteen lakhs . . . no wonder their Pujo is superior.'

'And how are we going to collect twelve lakhs, Biplab da?'

'That's easy. This year just demand twice of what someone paid last year. If someone gave five-hundred rupees last year, this year just demand a thousand . . . that's all.'

Partho scratched his ear and shook his head. It was easy for Biplab da to say these things. He never went about collecting *chanda*. Partho and his friends would have to do all the legwork. It was a nightmare trying to get even twenty rupees from some of the residents and Biplab da was dreaming of extracting a thousand!

The coming two months were going to be pretty rough.

★

Mrs Bose was every inch the gentle lady that Debdas Guha Roy and his wife had expected her to be. She seated herself on the larger sofa, and smiled sweetly at Piya (dressed in a blue silk sari, and seated on the chair beside the bookshelf). The prospective groom sat beside his mother.

Both mother and son were of a similar build – round and heavy, with a large round face and big round eyes that sported almost identical round glasses. If it hadn't been for the age difference, they could easily have passed off as siblings. Piya had been told by her mother, not to look directly at the boy. Now, stealing a glance at the prospective groom, Piya wondered if the boy too had received similar instructions from his mother.

'Mrs Bose, please feel free to ask Anamika anything you like,' insisted Chhaya Guha Roy.

'Anamika . . . such a sweet name. What are you called at home?' asked Mrs Bose, a sweet smile ever-present on her lips.

Piya decided to give her future husband some competition and joined him in staring at the floor. Chhaya Guha Roy shifted uneasily in her seat, 'She is feeling a little shy, didi.'

'Oh, of course. I understand. It is good to know that such children still exist. Most young boys and girls of today are so ill mannered and rude. You have raised your daughter very well Mrs Guha Roy.'

Chhaya Guha Roy smiled politely.

Debdas Guha Roy had used the formal pronoun *aapni* with the prospective groom, to which Mrs Bose protested vehemently. 'There is no need for such formality, Mr Guha Roy,' she said. 'Please address Gopal as *tumi*.' Debdas Guha Roy rephrased his question.

Gopal was about to answer the floor, when his mother volunteered, 'Procter and Gamble – it's a big MNC. He is working there for five years now.'

Hot pea-*kachauris* had been served. Mrs Bose protested mildly for politeness' sake, but helped herself to a few. Her son needed some coaxing, but eventually managed to gulp down a couple.

'So Anamika,' asked Mrs Bose, turning down the fifth kachauri that Chhaya Guha Roy was about to place on her plate, 'What are your hobbies? Can you sing?'

Piya was on her guard. Experience had taught her that if she answered 'yes' to the above question, she would immediately be asked to showcase her talent. She shook her head gently, all the time keeping her eyes on the red cemented floor.

'Piya has received training in semi classical vocal music, didi,' Chhaya Guha Roy hastened to minimize the damage done. 'She is just feeling a little shy, that's all.'

'Hmm,' smiled Mrs Bose. 'Can Anamika cook?' Mrs Bose asked, to which she got Piya's head shake again.

'Anamika has been so occupied with her studies, she never got an opportunity to help me in the kitchen,' offered Chhaya Guha Roy. 'But of course, now she will have to learn little by little.'

Mrs Bose nodded in comprehension.

'What are your interests, Gopal?' asked Chhaya Guha Roy before more questions could be directed at her daughter.

For a moment Piya wondered if Gopal would ever make his voice heard. He parted his lips slightly, but not a sound came out. In the seconds that followed Gopal racked his brains to find the words that best described his life's passions. The suspense was almost killing.

'He likes to read and watch TV,' offered his mother finally.

A few such queries later, it was evident that neither Anamika nor Gopal were willing to make their voices heard. The Guha Roys and Mrs Bose therefore did the talking for them.

'Where did Anamika go to school, Mrs Guha Roy?'

'Loreto Convent, didi. What about Gopal?'

'He went to Patha Bhaban.'

'What kind of music does Anamika like?'

'She likes Rabindra sangeet and Nazrul Geeti.' Piya winced.

'Oh? Gopal loves Rabindra sangeet too. And *Adhunik gaan* . . . don't you Gopal?'

Putting down her finished cup of tea, Mrs Bose looked at Piya and smiled approvingly.

'A very nice daughter you have Mrs Guha Roy. So gentle and well-mannered. From my side it is a yes. If it is not too hurried for you, I would like to fix a tentative date for the *ashirbaad*. You see, to come from Mumbai, it is not easy . . . one has to reserve train tickets days in advance. Then I have to inform all the relatives, they too have to make sure that they are free.'

Piya stared disbelievingly at her mother. So this was it? She had not spoken a single word with the boy, and she was already being married off to him? What year was this, 1929??

Piya stood up abruptly. Breathing hard, she looked at her parents and then at Mrs Bose. 'As much as you like me,' she blurted, 'I am afraid I cannot marry your son.'

Mrs Bose seemed more shocked at the revelation that her future daughter-in-law could actually speak!

'You see,' continued Piya, 'I am not the quiet, submissive girl you presume me to be. And I am definitely not marrying a boy, who has no say of his own. Please forgive me.'

She ran upstairs, locked herself in her room, threw herself on her bed and wept uncontrollably.

A Nightmare

The house in Bosepukur Road was bursting with people. Everyone was there . . . Boudi, Mejda, Bulai, Chhotka, Monu. What was the occasion? Looks like somebody is about to get married. People are running about ordering sweets and more cups of tea. Bibhuti Bose is busy as well, making sure the guests are being looked after. After all, everything was in his hands now. Now that Dada was no more.

But how could he take care of everything on his own? He was only 16. He still had two younger sisters to marry off. And what about Chhotka? Dada's 4 year old son? His entire life lay ahead of him. What about Boudi? He would have to take care of so many people, plus this marriage. He felt helpless . . . why did Dada have to go away so soon? The groom's family had arrived. Some boys lifted the bride on a low stool, and circled her around the groom. She hid her face with a pair of betel leaves, but she was pretty. He could tell. Then her face was revealed . . . why? It was Sona! Bibhuti Bose's own daughter! How quickly she had grown. If only Dada were here to see this day.

'I am here Buro, what are you worried about?'

Bibhuti Bose turned slowly, almost scared that he might wake up. 'Dada you came?'

He could control himself no longer. He hugged his older brother and sobbed uncontrollably, 'Dada, you came! Dada you are here!' Nothing else mattered anymore. It didn't matter that all the guests were staring at him . . . it didn't matter that . . . 'Wait! Dada why are you going away? Dada, wait!' He wanted to scream, but no words came out. He held on to his brother as tightly as he could, but Dada was getting away . . . I'll take care of Boudi and Chhotka, don't worry, he screamed.

All the guests had left. He was standing alone in the large hall. Wonder if Sona got married? Did the shehnai player come? Yes, there he was . . . But it was too shrill! Play it softly! That's not how you play the shehnai . . . it must be Raag Maru Behag. Stop!

'Wake up!,' Joyoti Bose's voice coupled with the shrill whistling of the security patrol, brought him back to reality.

Bibhuti Bose sat up, pulled up the mosquito net, and got out of bed. He walked over to the bathroom and splashed water on his face. Dada was here . . . He could still feel the warmth of his embrace. An inexplicable feeling welled up inside him. If only. . . .

He sighed and made his way to the kitchen. He put a betel leaf in his mouth, seated himself on the living room armchair, and switched on the TV. He flipped from one channel to the other. Which insomniac would want to buy a treadmill at this hour, so he could exercise early in the morning, he wondered. He continued the channel flipping for a while, and then gave up.

What did Dr Mullick know? He opened his medicine box and popped in a Valium tablet.

★

'I don't see Debdas babu today?' asked Chandan Mukherjee, settling down on the bench.

The air was humid. The leaves stood motionless. A bunch of crows, seated atop the gulmohar tree, cawed incessantly. It was only six in the morning, and yet the fine cotton *panjabis* stuck to their bodies as if they had been glued.

Akhil Banerjee wiped his forehead. 'Looks like there'll be a thunderstorm today. It's impossible to exercise in this weather, moshai.'

'Joj Saheb, I went to see Dr Mullick yesterday,' said Bibhuti Bose.

'Yes, did he say anything?'

'Well, you see. . .'

'Here comes Chaar Padabi!' called out Chandan Mukherjee hastily. 'Good morning, Debdas babu.'

'Good morning,' said Debdas Guha Roy as he walked towards the bench.

'How come you are so late today, Debdas babu?' asked Chandan Mukherjee.

'Did not sleep very well last night,' sighed Debdas Guha Roy as he sat down beside Chandan Mukherjee.

The tea-stall owner arrived with four earthen cups of tea. The gentlemen fished out coins from their pockets.

'Bibhuti babu, you were saying you met Dr Mullick?'

'Yes, I did,' Bibhuti Bose hesitated. He stole a glance at Chandan Mukherjee, who gave him forbidding looks. 'Well he. . .'

'What did he give you for the constipation, moshai?' asked Chandan Mukherjee. 'I'm having some trouble for the past two days.'

'Take some *isabgool*, Chandan babu,' suggested Debdas Guha Roy.

'*Durr, isabgool* doesn't work for me,' said Chandan Mukherjee.

'Then change your diet. Eat more leafy greens. Spinach is very good.'

'Can't. I have high uric acid, moshai. Cannot even complain about the food at home. My wife will make this *tadka daal* . . . Uff, Horrible!'

'What are you saying, moshai? Have you tasted the *tadka daal* of the *dhabas* on Diamond Harbour road? Aha—fantastic!' said Bibhuti Bose.

'May be you should walk a little,' suggested Akhil Banerjee. 'Anyways, Bibhuti babu, you were saying . . . about Dr Mullick?'

'Oh yes, well. . . .' hesitated Bibhuti Bose.

'It has to be Sujit, moshai,' asserted Chandan Mukherjee, taking a sip from his steaming cup.

'How can you be so sure, Chandan babu?' asked Akhil Banerjee.

'Why? By simple elimination, moshai. It wasn't the four of us. Dr Mullick will surely not take a ring . . . he has no dearth of money. He is a well-respected citizen. That only leaves Sujit, right? He is the only one who looked like he was in need of money.'

'I wouldn't eliminate everyone that easily,' stated Bibhuti Bose. 'It is difficult to understand human psychology, moshai. Don't you agree, Joj Saheb? It is not only dearth of money that makes one take things that do not belong to him.'

'What do you mean, Bibhuti babu?' asked Akhil Banerjee. Chandan Mukherjee coughed loudly.

'You hear of these things so often,' continued Bibhuti Bose unperturbed. 'Just the other day, a famous Hollywood actress was caught shoplifting from a New York departmental store. Do you think she had no money to pay for it?' Bibhuti Bose shook his head. 'Later she told the police that she was rehearsing for a role in a film. Imagine!'

'But that is a disease, moshai,' said Akhil Banerjee. 'Kleptomania . . . are you saying that is what happened here?'

'It very well may have. One never knows. . . .'

'The important thing is, we don't know where Sujit lives,' said Chandan Mukherjee. 'In any case, if he has the ring . . . which is the most likely possibility, he must have escaped by now.'

'Hmm, Rakshit came to see me the other day. His men went to Shucheta Cabin in Lake Market, but couldn't find anyone there Bibhuti babu.' He looked at Debdas Guha Roy. 'Are you alright, Debdas babu? You don't look so well.'

'Huh?' Debdas Guha Roy seemed to come out of his reverie. 'Oh . . . no, no it's nothing.' He sighed.

'What is it Debdas babu?' asked Chandan Mukherjee.

'Its . . . it's about Piya. I suppose every father with a grown-up daughter has to face this some day. You see, she is almost twenty-three. Sooner or later I will have to find a home for her. . . .'

Chandan Mukherjee gave him a pat on his back. 'Arrey, don't worry Debdas babu. The thing about marriages is that it will happen, wherever and whenever god has intended it to happen. There is no point in worrying about it. By god's grace, Piya is a smart, well-qualified, well-mannered girl. She will find a very good home, I'm sure of it. Don't worry!'

Debdas Guha Roy cheered up a little. 'Yes, yes I suppose you are right,' he said.

'As I was saying, the problem is tracking down Sujit,' said Chandan Mukherjee, as he got up to leave. The others got up as well. 'It's a pity the disappearance wasn't discovered while he was still there.'

★

Poltu scratched his mosquito-bitten arm and cursed under his breath. He had perched himself on top of the boundary wall of the Sabuj Kalyan Park. His scrawny legs dangled inches above the ground. It was not a particularly comfortable spot. The failing light brought about an army of mosquitoes that played the concerto all around him. He had to constantly shake a leg, wiggle his body, or flail his arms wildly about himself, in order to keep the mosquitoes at bay. Yet, in spite of his manoeuvres to counter the enemies, every once in a while, a mosquito would manage to land on an area of exposed skin, and even before Poltu could feel its menacing presence, would pierce his skin and draw his blood, only to be squashed the very next second.

Any passer-by would be baffled by why Poltu chose to spend this time of the day at this particular spot. But Poltu had his reasons. It was the time of the day he looked forward to the most. Not the mosquito bites. But the one thing that made all those bites bearable, even sweet. This was the time of the day he could catch a glimpse of the love of his life, his queen. This was when Piya Guha Roy returned home each day.

A disturbing thought had been troubling Poltu the past couple of weeks. Piya had returned earlier than usual on two separate days. That in itself was not worrisome, except that on both those days, taxis had pulled up in front of her home, and well-dressed strangers holding packets of sweets had gotten out of them. Could it be that they had come to 'see' Piya?

The thought had paralysed Poltu, and robbed him of his sleep. His Piya, the girl he dreamed about day and night, being married off to another man. Poltu had done what any man in his frame of mind would have done. He had brooded. This was followed by a day of deep introspection.

He had the looks, Poltu was sure of it. He was tall, dark and according to his best friend Bhombol, possessed mirror-shattering looks. Poltu was not one to believe whatever his friends told him. So he would spend several hours each day in front of the mirror, combing his hair this way and that, squinting his eyes, flexing his facial muscles and checking out his profile. A couple of unsightly pimples had erupted quite unexpectedly on his otherwise smooth cheeks, but he was applying generous doses of Clearasil ointment borrowed from his sister, on them.

Sure he had never actually spoken to Piya, but that was a mere technicality. He could speak to her anytime he wanted. He was just waiting for the right moment. In his mind he had rehearsed the scene thoroughly. He would approach Piya, hold her hands, look her in the eye, and in that confident, lecherous voice that Hindi film heroes use, to win their lady-loves, would say the words, 'Piya, I love you!'

Piya would naturally throw herself in his arms. They might sing and dance in the rain. Her family, being the rich, educated types, might create a ruckus. But what's a little obstacle in the face of true love? They would elope if necessary, and get married on a temple atop a hill far away, long before her parents could arrive there to foil the marriage.

The story was perfectly scripted. The only problem was getting started. He sighed and waved off an insect buzzing near his face.

'What's up, Poltu?' hollered Bhombol, appearing out of nowhere. 'What are you doing here?'

'Ah . . . nothing.'

'Nothing?' said Bappa, who came up behind Bhombol. 'Then come to the Pujo meeting. Biplab da is waiting.'

'Ah . . . tell him I'll be late.'

'Why? You said you were doing nothing.'

'I'm just . . .waiting.'

'For what?' asked Bhombol.

'Rather, for whom?' asked Bappa, a sly smile appearing on his lips as he glanced up the street.

Poltu fidgeted nervously.

'You guys go ahead. I'll join you in a few minutes.'

'I think I'll wait too,' said Bappa, hoisting himself onto the wall.

'Arrey, no, no,' protested Poltu. 'I don't want you guys to be late because of me. Just go ahead, and I'll catch up.'

Bappa dismissed the idea.

'That's out of the question, Poltu. After all we are your friends. Bhombol hoist yourself up here. Careful, don't bring down the wall.'

Bhombol did as he was told. Getting his hefty body to do as he desired wasn't easy. It took him several attempts, and finally with the help of Poltu he managed to bring himself onto the top of the wall.

They sat silently for several minutes. Bhombol and Bappa were warding off mosquitoes on either side of Poltu, and for a brief second Poltu decided it was a good thing that his friends were there after all. Soon impatience got the better of Bappa. He whistled a tune, and when a young girl passed them by, quickly filled the melody with lyrics of a love song. It was just one of those things that Bhombol and Poltu admired about Bappa. He had guts, that boy.

'What do you guys think of Biplab da's plan this year?' asked Bhombol, when the humming had died down.

'Spectacular!' replied Bappa tilting his head to one side. 'If we can pull it off, that is.'

'But the lion and the peacock. . . ?'

'That's the shock effect! Who would expect a live lion in the pandal of Ma Durga, tell me? Besides I think he has already contacted a friend from Gemini Circus. They will lend us the lion at a discounted price. Poltu, are you coming with us tomorrow for chanda collection? Poltu?'

Poltu wasn't listening. His eyes were focused at a point in front of him. Bappa and Bhombol followed his gaze. There in the flickering light of the lamp-post, a woman appeared, as if from a haze. She walked gracefully, almost glided on the pot-holed street, her long, luxurious braided hair, swinging behind her back, her orange dupatta flung carelessly over her slender shoulders. She walked unhurriedly, though she checked her watch often. She came within a few feet of the gaping threesome. And then abruptly, almost cruelly, without so much as a glance in their direction, turned and walked towards Haripada Das Lane.

Poltu let out a long sigh, and squashed the two mosquitoes which had been feasting on his immobile arm for the past few seconds.

'Show's over, boys,' said Bappa, slapping Poltu on the back. 'Let's get to the club house.'

An Idea

'Arrey, sir? Why did you bother? You could have simply telephoned . . . I could have come over to your house, sir.'

'It's alright, Rakshit. I know you have a lot to do . . . I cannot simply ask you to leave your work to come see me?' Akhil Banerjee settled down in the chair offered to him. A junior constable was asked to fetch tea, but Akhil Banerjee politely refused.

'Tell me sir. What can I do for you?'

'Hmm . . . nothing really. I was wondering if you had any new information about the Agarwal theft.'

'Oh that!' Sudarshan Rakshit sighed and clicked his tongue. 'It's an open and shut case, sir. Sujit (if that is his real name) took the ring and escaped. As I told you, we sent our men to Shucheta Cabin . . . no luck! To my mind he escaped from the city even before the disappearance was discovered. By now, he would have sold it off and be revelling in his good fortune, It's a pity that the theft was not noticed earlier . . . we would have surely nabbed him.'

'Hmm . . . I see. So are you saying that you have washed your hands off the case?'

'Sir, under the circumstances there is nothing much I can do. Looking for Sujit is like looking for a needle in a haystack. We don't even know what he really looks like . . . in all likelihood the beard and the moustache were false. Under these circumstances. . . .'

'Hmm, I see,' Akhil Banerjee got up. 'Anyway Rakshit . . . thanks for your time'. He got up and then turned to leave. 'Rakshit?' He hesitated.

'Sir?'

'I was wondering . . . can you do me a favour?'

'Anything, sir.'

Akhil Banerjee thought for a minute. 'Do you know of any other case involving Mr Agarwal? I mean the man has many curio items . . . has anything like this ever occurred before?'

Sudarshan Rakshit curved his lips in a lopsided smile. 'I see you still haven't given up, sir. Once a Judge, always a Judge . . . what do you say? Ha, ha.' He laughed heartily. 'Well, I can surely find out. He used to live in Bhowanipore before coming here. I will contact the ACP there and ask him.'

'Very good. Thank you, Rakshit.'

'You are welcome, sir. And don't worry . . . as soon as I have some news, I will come over myself to inform you, sir.'

'Thank you again. Good day to you.'

'Good day, sir.'

★

'You listening?' called out Kalpana Mukherjee, straining to make her voice heard over the sound of the exhaust fan in the kitchen.

'Yes, yes,' replied Chandan Mukherjee. 'I'm just leaving.'

'Wait a minute!' called out his wife. 'I forgot to mention two things in the list. *Dhoney paata* and *gandharaj lebu*.' (Coriander leaves and scented lime.)

'*Tej paata* and *saabu*?' (Bay leaves and sagu?)

'Yes, yes. Coriander leaves and lime. Write it down on the list in case you forget.'

'Why will I forget? How difficult is it to remember two simple things?'

'Alright, then. Come back quickly, the cook will be here any minute.'

★

The doorbell in Bibhuti Bose's house rang a second time. He clicked his tongue in impatience and cast aside the newspaper with mild irritation. He pulled himself out of the reclining chair with some effort, and made his way to the door, unhurriedly, his flip-flops clapping against the black and white chequered floor. He had just about reached the front door when the bell rang once more.

'I'm coming. I'm coming,' he called out.

Standing outside the threshold were the weather-beaten faces of Partho, Somen, Bappa and Jishu.

'What is it?'

'Chanda,' replied Partho. 'We are collecting funds for this year's Pujo.' His voice, as always, was a few decibels higher than was strictly required.

'Already?'

'Yes, kaku. There is a lot to do this year.'

'How much?' asked Bibhuti Bose with disinterest.

'1000.'

'1000 rupees?? Have you gone mad? Last year I gave 500. I have the receipt if you don't believe me.'

'Yes, yes kaku. It is not a question of not believing you. But prices increase each year. Surely you know that. . . .'

'Besides we have grand plans for this year!' piped in Somen.

'What grand plans?'

'You'll see kaku . . . it's unlike anything you have ever seen.'

Bibhuti Bose pondered over it for a moment.

'We are in a hurry, kaku. Have to go to all the houses in this lane today,' Partho sounded impatient.

'Let me think about it Partho. Come back next week.'

'Next week??' yelled Somen, loudly enough for the neighbours to hear. 'Why kaku? You know we have so much to do, so many things. . . .'

'Yes, yes, of course. You are doing a lot!' replied Bibhuti Bose, the sarcasm unmistakable in his retort.

'Kaku, why are you creating a fuss?' asked Partho, lowering his voice.

'Fuss? I am not creating a fuss. Who says I'm creating a fuss? Please go now. I have things to do.'

Somen was about to protest, when Partho slammed shut his receipt book and motioned to his coterie to follow him, muttering obscenities under his breath, that Bibhuti Bose obliterated by slamming the door shut.

★

'*Ei ki*?' cried out Kalpana Mukherjee, fishing out items from the nylon *tholi*, the grocery bag. 'Who asked you to bring bay leaves and sagu?'

'Bah! You did!'

'When? Have you gone completely mad? I asked you to get coriander leaves and lime. For the *masoor dal* that Tubai likes so much.'

'If you wanted coriander leaves and lime you should have said so. I could have gotten them in addition to the barley and bay leaves.'

'Uff! I never asked for . . . ' she stopped and shook her head. 'I don't even know why I bother telling you anything. You never listen anyway.'

'What is the problem in saying things clearly?' retorted Chandan Mukherjee, as he climbed the stairs.

He settled down on his armchair and lit a cigarette. On his right hand he held the detective novel, borrowed from the collection of his younger son. It was an intriguing case, about the owner of a theatre company who had been murdered. All the actors in his company were suspects. They all had ample opportunity. And each one had a personal grudge against the owner. Any one of them could have done it.

Now if this same detective was asked to solve the Agarwal case, what would he do? In novels it was somehow always easier. All the clues were there, and then it was simply a question of connecting the dots. He wondered. . . .

★

Akhil Banerjee came out of the Jadavpur police station, crossed the road to his white ambassador parked in the opposite lane.

'*Kahan jana hain*, sir. Where to?' asked his chauffeur, as soon as he climbed in.

Akhil Banerjee did not seem to hear the question. He was lost in thought.

'Sir?' the chauffeur asked again. 'Where would you like to go?' he repeated.

'Oh . . . let' go home,' he said. They had barely made a U-Turn when he spotted Debdas Guha Roy, on the footpath, struggling with heavy bags.

'*Ei* Balram, stop, stop,' said Akhil Banerjee to his chauffeur. 'Debdas babu!' he called out. '*Edikey*, come this way,' he motioned.

Debdas Guha Roy zigzagged his way through a maze of cars and buses waiting at the signal. Balram got out of the car to open the door for him. He took the packets from Debdas Guha Roy and placed them in front, next to the driver's seat.

'Thank you, Joj Saheb,' said Debdas Guha Roy as he wiped his forehead. 'It is so difficult to get a taxi these days, especially for short distances. Have been waiting at the bus stop for almost twenty minutes. Buses are so crowded this time of the day, I couldn't manage to get up with these heavy packets.'

'Looks like more books?'

'Yes you are right. Had gone to College Street early this morning. I know a book seller there. He calls me whenever there is a good supply of rare books. I received a call from him two weeks ago, moshai. But with everything that has been going on lately, did not quite find the time to go.'

'Hmm . . . I went to see Sudarshan Rakshit today. Seems like they are not going to investigate the Agarwal case anymore.'

'Oh, I see. . .'

'How's your daughter, Debdas babu? I apologize I forgot her name.'

'I have two, Joj Saheb. Piya is the older one. I think she is the one you are asking about. She's fine Joj Saheb.'

'And your other daughter? What's her name?'

'Diya. She is in class XII. She will appear for her *ucchya madhyamik* exams next year.'

'Good, good. Don't worry, Debdas babu. I'm sure you will find a nice boy for Piya. After all, there is no dearth of qualified Bengali boys in the country.'

'I hope so, Joj Saheb. I hope so.'

The car entered Uday Shankar Sarani.

'Joj Saheb, you can drop me off here. No need to take the car all the way to Haripada Das Lane.'

'Arrey no no. Balram, go to Haripada Das Lane. Debdas babu, tell him the way to your house, please.'

'Joj Saheb, it will be difficult for you to make a U-turn afterwards. . .' protested Debdas Guha Roy, but the car was already in his lane. He pointed to the house with the green gate, and motioned the driver to stop.

'Joj Saheb, come in for a cup of tea. You have never visited my house. What do you say?'

'Some other day, Debdas babu, surely.'

'Alright. Thank you so much Joj Saheb. Really lucky to have run into you.'

Balram helped him with the packets, before driving away.

Debdas Guha Roy entered his house, took off his shoes, and deposited the packets on a table nearby.

'Our Joj Saheb is a wonderful gentleman,' he said smiling broadly.

'Why do you say that?' asked his wife, folding the washed clothes and bundling them for the ironing-man, the *istri-wallah*.

'Na, I'm just saying . . . He saw me near the Jadavpur bus stop and gave me a ride. He needn't have come all the way to our house really. I told him it would be difficult to get his car out of the lane, but he wouldn't listen.'

'O Ma! Joj Saheb came to our house, and you didn't invite him in?'

'I did, I did. But he promised he would come some other time.'

The phone rang. Diya went to answer it.

'Baba, it's for you.'

'Hello,' Debdas Guha Roy spoke into the receiver.

'Hello, Debdas babu? Chandan Mukherjee here.'

'Yes, Chandan babu, tell me. What can I do for you?'

'I just thought of something. The other day when we were at the park, do you remember one of your students came to speak to you?'

'Umm . . . which one?'

'Arrey, the one who is a script-writer for Bengali TV serials. What was his name?'

'Oh ho. Khokon. Why do you ask?'

'Well, I was just wondering . . . if this Sujit had a false beard and moustache maybe he has an easy access to these things. Is it not possible that he works in a theatre company, or maybe on the sets of a television or film production company?'

'*Arribbas*! Good thinking, moshai. But what do you want from Khokon?'

'I was just thinking that maybe he can give us the names of the local production companies. Then we could go and have a look, what do you say?'

'Hmm . . . I see. Okay, let me see if I can contact him. I'll keep you posted.'

'Thank you, Debdas babu.'

'No problem, Sir.'

'What did Chandan Babu want?' asked Chhaya Guha Roy as soon as her husband replaced the receiver.

'Oh, nothing.'

'Nothing? I heard you say you were going to meet Khokon? Who is Khokon?'

'Arrey, no one,' said Debdas Guha Roy and he quickly slipped into his study with his packets and shut the door.

★

It was Pujo once more. The house in Bosepukur Road was brimming with people. All the children were there. They crowded around Bibhuti Bose, their faces alit with expectations.

After all it was Durga Pujo.

'Chhoto kaka, what have you brought for me?'

'Chhoto mama, what have you brought for me?'

Bibhuti Bose had gifts for everyone. He did not know where the money had come from. It didn't matter. The important thing was that everyone was going to be happy. No one should feel deprived just because Dada was no more. He took out the presents one by one; a pink dress for Monu, a red one for Bula, saris for his sisters, and shiny new boots for Chhotka, just like the ones he had admired on the window of the Bata showroom. They were all admiring their gifts . . . no one bothered to ask Bibhuti Bose if he had bought something for himself. Anyway, it did not matter . . . as long as they were all happy.

The children were saying something, he couldn't hear them properly. 'Chhoto mama, you are great! Chhoto kaka, we love you!' The voices got louder and louder . . . almost like a chant.

But wait! That's not what they were really saying. Chhotka was saying, 'Chhoto kaka, you are hopeless. I asked for red boots, you bought black ones. These look old and cheap.' He screamed and hurled his pair of boots across the room. The others joined him. They were all throwing their gifts away. Bibhuti Bose asked them to stop but no one was listening. Chhotka was now making faces at him, and calling him names. Obscene names . . . how could a boy of his age use such profanity? Everyone was pointing fingers at Bibhuti Bose and laughing at him. He implored them to stop. More people joined them . . . some faces he could not even recognize. There was Partho, Somen, and Bappa. Partho took out a whistle from his pocket and blew hard. It was a loud, shrill noise . . . STOOOP!! He screamed and sat up on his bed.

Lightning flashed, followed by the rumbling of thunder. Rain lashed heavily against the window pains.

Joyoti Bose flicked on the light. 'Water?'

Bibhuti Bose nodded. He rubbed his eyes with his palms, pulled up the mosquito net and got off the bed. He felt for his flip-flops with his toes.

'Why do you think about terrible things before going to bed? Why don't you try reading a nice book instead?'

Bibhuti Bose stole a glance at his wife. 'Do you?'

'You kept calling out to Chhotka,' she said handing him a glass of water. 'Why do you concern yourself with people who don't give a damn whether you are dead or alive?'

Bibhuti Bose sighed heavily. She was right. If he were to die today, Chhotka wouldn't even bother to come to his funeral. He smiled to himself. It was a sad smile. The things he had done for this family! How easily people forget. . . .

Bad News, Biplab Da

Chhaya Guha Roy glanced at the morning paper with mild interest. A Nepali sherpa was attempting to climb the Mount Everest without oxygen cylinders, a Frenchman was attempting to cross the Atlantic in a sail boat. Apart from that there was the war against terror, of course. One could hardly look at news these days without coming across a war, in some form or the other.

What was it that made people fight, she wondered. Ideologies, land, power? How could any of these be more important than a human life? Ideology, now that could change any day, couldn't it? One heard of these stories so often; a communist had become a priest in a temple, a Hindu had become a Christian. Just look at the ministers. One moment they would be screaming themselves hoarse about how the other party was looting the public, and later when convenient, would hug each other and pose for front-page photographs. When it came to ideologies, she thought, it was just a matter of time, before you found something else more appealing, more interesting.

Land, it seemed, was one thing worth killing for. A small piece of earth, mingled with dust and sweat. How much of land did one need really? Yet historically, didn't all wars start because of land? Kings would invade other kingdoms to acquire more land, which would ultimately give them more power. More power to do what? Wouldn't they be doing pretty much the same things as before? Eating, drinking, watching dancing girls, flying pigeons or kites? What did they want really? More pigeons?

Trade and commerce was an important factor, of course. Reigning over a larger territory gave the kings more power to control trade, which ultimately brought more to their coffers. War in modern times too, was motivated by the same principles, sighed Chhaya Guha Roy. Did a government really care about the well-being of the common man in an alien nation, and strive to free its people from their oppressors? Only if getting involved served an economic purpose.

These people who could not tolerate another with different beliefs, or who fought with each other on various pretexts, what were they looking for really? Happiness, thought Chhaya Guha Roy. Wasn't that ironic? Somewhere in their minds, is a belief that acquiring this and achieving that will bring them happiness. Wasn't that the driving force behind every action? For some, happiness meant climbing the highest peak or crossing the Atlantic, for some it meant winning a war, thwarting one's enemies, and for some like herself, it meant watching her children grow up to be good, kind, human beings and finding them a good home to settle down in.

Once, while in college, Chhaya Guha Roy had been writing an interpretation of a Jibananda Das poem, and it had struck her that the words *khushi* (happy) and *sukhi* (contented), had almost the same letterings in Bengali and had very similar meanings. Yet, happiness, she thought, was eternally tied to various blobs of events that occurred from time to time in one's life. Events, the details of which had faded, only the memory that it had been a good, happy time, had remained. The time when I had won the music contest, I was happy. The time I had got a new dress, I was happy. The day I became a mother, I was happy. But, contentment was beyond happiness, she had thought, a state of being that was beyond a mere 'feeling'. A state, when one felt that everything was just right, everything was perfect, and absolutely nothing needed to be changed. She recounted how many contented people she knew, and was disturbed to find that the answer was none. Didn't one always hear people crib about their jobs, or their relationships, or the inflation rate, or some sickness or the other? It was one of those human weaknesses, she had decided. No matter what you had, you always wanted more or at least something else.

Some months later, while holidaying in Gangtok with her family, she had seen a bust of the Buddha, eyes closed, a soft smile on his lips. It seemed to say, I don't care how beautiful the Himalayas look from here, I am happy to sit here with my eyes closed. She had at once known what that look had meant.

Contentment.

★

'We have bad news, Biplab da,' Partho's tone was grave. He and his friends were seated on the floor, legs spread out in front of them.

'Hmm,' sighed Biplab da. He was seated on the desk, legs dangling inches above the floor. His head hung, as if in agony of the defeat that stared him in the eye. His fingers tapped an irregular beat on the edge of the desk.

'Hmm,' he repeated.

The silence that followed was unnerving. Partho, Pinaki, Somen, Bhombol, Poltu, Bappa and Jishu were like a bunch of injured soldiers returning from the battlefield. They expected Biplab da to shout at them, call them worthless nincompoops, and order them to march back to the war zone again. This silence, however, was too much to handle.

'Say something, Biplab da,' coaxed Jishu.

In response, Biplab da only hummed a tune from an old Hindi song, along with the tapping. It was a sad song, something about the pangs of agony due to betrayed love. The boys looked at each other. What was happening to their leader? The one man inspiration who had pulled out many a *pujo* at the last moment by sheer will power and determination, the captain of the local cricket team, who had hit a sixer off the last ball to win the Agragami tournament, so crestfallen, so heartbroken!

'No, no, Biplab da, why are you losing heart?' blurted Somen, unable to take it any longer. 'There is still one more month left. We will be able to do it, I promise you.'

The others murmured similar thoughts.

'Somen is right,' continued Partho. 'Arrey this happens every year, doesn't it? No one wants to pay chanda until the last moment. People try to put it off for as long as they can. They don't understand that we have to make advance payments to the decorators, the lighting people. . . .'

'You know the problem with this neighbourhood?' offered Bappa. 'It is like an old age home. Don't you think? All the oldies live here. And they are all so old-fashioned, so out of touch with modern times. . . .'

'Correct, Bappa!' seconded Pinaki. 'And they are all so afraid of parting with their money. Remember when we went to Sanyal babu's house? Old man in his 80s . . . might die any day now. Lives alone in his old house . . . stinking rich!' He joined the tips of his fingers and threw the invisible object it held. It was the gesture that was meant to convey any extreme. 'Yet, when he heard the chanda amount, he almost had a heart attack. What does he think? He will carry all the money to heaven with him?'

'And all of them are like that,' continued Bappa. 'Bibhuti Bose – Not today. Come tomorrow. Now I'm busy, come next week.' Bappa mimicked. 'Arrey you are going to give the money eventually. Why delay it unnecessarily?'

'And look at Milonee. Their neighbourhood has all the smart young professionals. I bet their boys don't have to do half the work we do,' finished Pinaki.

'I have some money left over from last month's bridge tournament,' offered Partho. 'I was saving it for a tape recorder, but Pujo comes first.'

Hopes and suggestions started pouring in from the most unlikely corners. Jishu offered to sell off his bicycle. Bhombol offered to set up a chaat and puchka stall, and donate all the profits to the Pujo. The enthusiasm was infectious.

'We have such a grand vision for this year, your vision Biplab da. Are we just going to give it up like that and let Milonee win again?' asked Somen. 'We will make it happen! As long as I have breath in this body, I will make sure that the Pujo happens in our club.' He thumped his chest to emphasize his loyalty. 'This will be a Pujo like no other, I give you my word. Tomorrow we will go to Uday Shankar Sarani again. Let me see how many of them refuse to pay up.' A swearing or two followed.

Biplab looked up to face the boys. What would happen to them if he quit now? What would happen to them, if Durga Pujo, the one thing that gave their life any purpose, any meaning, was taken away from them? No, that simply could not be allowed to happen. He, Biplab Maity would see to it. He looked lovingly at the boys; his boys . . . all fired up and ready to give all it took. An uncomfortable lump had lodged itself in his throat. He tried his best to gulp it down.

★

The boy's family was here to see Sona again. They had already approved of her of course. This was just a formality. Apart from Bibhuti Bose, Joyoti Bose, Sona and the boy's parents, Akhil Banerjee, Debdas Guha Roy and Chandan Mukherjee were also present. They were all sitting there, enjoying the snacks and tea. Debdas Guha Roy got up suddenly and walked over to the almirah. Bibhuti Bose's heart began to pound. All of Sona's wedding jewellery was in that almirah. How many times had he told Joyoti to remove it to the locker? Even before he could shout out to Debdas Guha Roy, he had turned the handle of the lock . . . Bibhuti Bose tried to stop him. It was proving to be very difficult. The room was suddenly very big, and it was taking him forever to reach Debdas Guha Roy. He kept bumping into furniture. Debdas Guha Roy had opened the door, when Bibhuti Bose made a dive for it. . . .

CHOR, CHOR, THIEF, THIEF!!

'What happened? What happened?' shrieked Joyoti Bose, as she fumbled with the flashlight. 'What thief? Where?'

Bibhuti Bose opened his eyes briefly.

'It's nothing. I was dreaming. Go back to sleep.'

He turned sides, and started snoring again.

★

'Moshai? Didn't see you at the park this morning?' Debdas Guha Roy called out, as he took back the change from the vegetable vendor. 'Got up late I suppose?'

'Slept late, you could say,' replied Bibhuti Bose, as he handed his nylon sack to Bishu.

'Hmm . . . how is your constipation?'

Bibhuti Bose contorted his face in response. The two of them made their way toward the fish sellers.

'Have they been to your house yet?' Bibhuti Bose asked indicating toward Partho and Bappa, who were haggling with a vendor only a few feet away.

'No, not yet. I hear they are making arbitrary demands now?'

'*Arrey* moshai. Why do you ask? They asked for a 1000 from me. Last year I had given 500. . . .'

'1000 rupees??' Debdas Guha Roy raised his eyebrows in incredulity. 'Moshai, I cannot afford it. I have so many expenses coming up now. Looking for a match for Piya . . . everything is so expensive these days. After all I am a retired professor. It is different for some others with hidden black money.'

'It's not for me, either,' said Bibhuti Bose. 'For middle-class Bengali families, expenses are already so high. Now with the interest-rates falling steadily. . . .'

'True, moshai.'

'Any progress in the Agarwal case? Did Joj Saheb say anything new today?'

'Joj Saheb did not come to the park either. It was just me and Chandan babu. By the way, Chandan babu has come up with an idea. It may be worth exploring.'

Debdas Guha Roy recounted to Bibhuti Bose his earlier conversation with Chandan Mukherjee.

'*Achha*, Debdas babu, why do you think people steal?' asked Bibhuti Bose when his friend finished narrating.

'Why? For money, mostly.'

'Yes, but what about people who already have enough?'

'Enough is only subjective moshai. What is enough for you and me, may not be so for another person. Bigger house, better car . . . is there any end to wants?'

'Hmm . . . you are right. *Ei* Nimai, what is the rate of hilsa today?'

'250 rupees a kilo, babu.'

'My god it seems Bengalis have to give up eating fish altogether.' Bibhuti Bose turned his attention back to Debdas Guha Roy.

'You know, Debdas babu, sometimes people do things without realizing what the actions might amount to. I once had a friend in college, Sudhir, who had a fascination for fine-nib pens. He might be admiring my gold nib Parker, and then without even realizing it he would slip it into his pocket. In the meantime I would be searching frantically (the pen belonged to my father, you see), and Sudhir would even help me look for the lost pen. And it would eventually turn up in his *panjabi* pocket! This happened more than once . . . believe it or not! Of course Sudhir used to be very embarrassed about the whole thing. It used to be an unconscious act on his part.'

Debdas Guha Roy laughed a hearty laugh.

'I see you still have not given up on the kleptomaniac theory, Bibhuti babu.'

'It is always possible, is it not?'

The two of them had come out of the market, and had turned to Haripada Das Lane.

'Come, Bibhuti babu, my house is just around the corner. Come in for a cup of tea. How long has it been since you dropped by?'

The Agony of Pet Names

Poltu was unusually distracted today. He had forced himself to attend the Pujo meeting, and judging from the animated way in which his fellow club member spoke, it was a crucial one. But try as he might, Poltu could not bring himself to focus on the evening's proceedings. His mind floated to Piya. His Piya.

In recent times, doubts of an unbearable nagging nature had cropped up in his mind. Was it possible that he was not nearly as dashing as he thought himself to be? He was tempted to brush this aside.

His evenings, perched atop the Sabuj Kalyan boundary wall, were turning out to be predictable. He would wait there, sometimes for two hours (for Piya changed her schedule often these days) and endure blood-sucking mosquitoes for most of that time. And when she came, she would always turn straight to Haripada Das Lane, without so much as a glance in his direction. If only she would look at him once, she would see what a prize catch he was. But no, it appeared, Poltu was forced to admit to himself, that Piya did not even know that he existed.

What was making matters worse these days, was the presence of his friends (if he could still call them that), Bappa and Bhombol. Both of them would appear minutes before Piya arrived and would talk loudly or laugh aloud at a ridiculous joke. Perhaps Piya was being put off by their loud voices and raucous laughter. And to make things worse, they would call out his name Poltu! Poltu! loud enough for the whole neighbourhood to hear. What kind of a name was that anyway? Which self-respecting girl would want a Poltu for a boyfriend? What could his mother be thinking? Sometimes Bappa and Bhombol, would unwittingly use other terms of endearment; Potol – that scrawny looking unappetizing vegetable that one had during diarrhoea, or Potla – a shapeless bundle. It was clear, whatever leverage he was getting from his looks, was being completely obliterated by his pet-name.

Bengali pet names really could make or break a man's life, he decided. There was his best friend, Bhombol. Could a boy named Bhombol be anything but pudgy? The very name implied a rolling mass of some sort. Then there was Kaltu, the dark one. Years of applying Fair and Lovely, would do nothing to change his complexion or his self-image. Bappa was marginally better. No wonder he could whistle at girls so effortlessly.

The meeting seemed to be nearing its end. Some of the boys were already standing up.

'Boys, tomorrow we are doing Haripada Das Lane,' announced Partho. 'Who is coming?'

At the mention of Haripada Das Lane, Poltu seemed to wake up.

'Haripada Das Lane?' he asked. 'Can I come along?' He was half hoping to be turned down, but Partho seemed pleased at getting a volunteer.

'Sure. Come along. The more the merrier,' he said.

★

'*Arrey*, I see Debdas babu has joined Joj Saheb for the morning walk today?' called out Chandan Mukherjee, as he approached the duo, tapping his walking stick lightly on the ground as he walked. His starched white dhuti-panjabi swayed gently in the cool morning breeze.

'The weather is so much better now after the rains. Why don't you join us, Chandan babu?' asked Akhil Banerjee.

Chandan Mukherjee smiled, raised his hand in a mild surrender, mumbled something about arthritis, and settled down on the bench. Debdas Guha Roy and Akhil Banerjee finished a few more rounds and joined him.

Debdas Guha Roy called out to the tea-stall owner and gestured 'three' with his fingers.

'Chandan babu, I was just telling Joj Sahib of your idea. He agrees that the police should have checked the local theatres.'

'It's definitely worth a try,' nodded Akhil Banerjee. 'Good thinking, Chandan babu.'

Chandan Mukherjee straightened his back. 'I was just reading a detective book, when this thought struck me . . . heh heh.'

The tea arrived.

'And I spoke to Khokon,' said Debdas Guha Roy as he produced a slip of paper from his pocket. 'Here'. He handed the list to his friends.

'*Baap re!* Fast work, Debdas babu,' said Akhil Banerjee as he and Chandan Mukherjee glanced through the list.

'Didn't he want to know why you were asking for this?'

'Yes, but I just told him it's for a student of mine, who wants to be an actor. That's all. He has promised me a guided tour anytime I visit.'

'Okay then, let's do this,' said Akhil Banerjee. 'I will go to Satyam Theatres today around ten. Would you like to check out Technician's Studio?' he asked his friends.

'I can't go today, moshai,' apologised Debdas Guha Roy. 'I have two tuitions this morning.'

'No problem,' said Chandan Mukherjee. 'Let me see if I can catch Bibhuti babu in the market.'

'How come he is not here today?' asked Akhil Banerjee, glancing at his watch and getting up. The others got up as well.

'*Arrey* moshai, he takes sleeping tablets every night. God knows why he has trouble sleeping,' said Chandan Mukherjee.

'Oh, by the way,' said Debdas Guha Roy, as they neared Haripada Das Lane. 'Have you noticed our new club house?'

'New club house? Where?' asked Chandan Mukherjee. Both he and Akhil Banerjee turned around, but the club house was not visible any more.

'Well, it's still the old club house, but with a new name.'

'Really? Hadn't noticed. So what is it called now?' asked Akhil Banerjee.

'Sabuj Kalyan Yuva Samiti. Sabuj Kalyan Youth Association.'

★

'Ma, have you seen my library book?' demanded Tubai, racing down the stairs. 'Ma? Ma?'

Kalpana Mukherjee switched off the exhaust fan in the kitchen. 'What are you screaming for?' she asked her younger son.

'I was asking, have you seen my library book? I have to return it today and I can't find it anywhere.'

'What's it called?'

'*Murder at Prithviraj Theatres.* Have you seen it?'

'No, I haven't. Ask your brother.'

Tubai ran up the stairs. He was about to barge into his brother's room, when he saw a hand-written sign stuck on the door with sellotape. Do not Disturb.

Tubai glanced at his watch, hesitated a few seconds, and knocked gently on the door.

'Dada?' he asked.

For a few seconds there was no response. Tubai knocked again, a little louder this time.

'Dada?'

'What is it?' asked his older brother from inside.

'Can I come in?'

'No.'

'Dada?'

'What do you want?'

'Have you seen my library book?'

'Have you seen the sign on the door?'

'Please, dada,' pleaded Tubai. 'I'm getting late. The title is *Murder at Prithviraj Theatres.* Have you seen it?'

'No, now get lost!'

For a moment Tubai was tempted to throw open the door and discover the reason for his brother's frequent strange behaviour. He glanced at his wristwatch. Perhaps another time, he thought. He was already very late.

★

The sign outside the La Paris Hair-Cutting Saloon, situated at the corner of Daily Market, said 'Come here for Best Hair-Cut and Die'. Its interior walls were decorated with posters of several Hollywood and Bollywood actors. Some of the posters were even autographed.

"Thank you, La Paris," Brad Pitt had written on his poster. "Best haircut in town," said Tom Cruise. Bollywood stars too had generously praised their services.

The reason why Bibhuti Bose, inspite of the foreboding sign outside, preferred to come here for a cut, was that it had an air conditioner which actually worked, and loyal customers got a free head massage. Now, feeling suitably pampered by Raju, who had given an extra five minutes of massage upon request, Bibhuti Bose, stepped outside into the blazing sun.

'Bibhuti babu!' called out Chandan Mukherjee. 'How come I didn't see you at the market today?'

'I went to Lake Market today, moshai. Got the best parshey fish.'

'Oh I see. Listen Bibhuti babu, we have some work to do,' said Chandan Mukherjee. He looked this way and that to make sure no one was within earshot, then motioned Bibhuti Bose to go with him under the shade of the tamarind tree. He recounted the discussion of the morning with Akhil Banerjee and Debdas Guha Roy.

'So would you come with me to the Technician's Studio? I plan on going there around eleven today.'

'Of course, of course!' said Bibhuti Bose excitedly. 'Just let me take a quick shower, and I'll meet you here in half an hour.'

In Search of A Criminal

Akhil Banerjee glanced at the address written on the piece of paper, and squinted at the numbers on the street . . . 38 . . . 39 . . . 'Ah there it is . . . 42! Balram find a parking somewhere here.'

He got off, slipped the paper into his pocket, slung the cloth bag on his shoulder, and walked up the steps of an old building, the yellow paint of which was peeling off in places. The cobweb covered signboard, painted by an artist of moderate talent, had the words Satyam Theatres; Estd. 1978, written on it. Akhil Banerjee rang the bell and waited. Presently, a young man in his mid twenties, with a long face and a thin moustache, appeared.

'Who do you want?' he asked in a gruff voice.

'Uh . . . umm . . . I'm here to see the manager of Satyam Theatres.'

'What for?'

'That, I will discuss with him.'

'Hmm . . . Okay. Wait here.'

The man went inside. He did not shut the door on Akhil Banerjee's face, but left it slightly ajar, which was the polite thing to do. Akhil Banerjee cursed himself for not having called earlier and taken an appointment. What if the manager wasn't available today?

The young man returned after about five minutes, and asked Akhil Banerjee to follow him. They went up a flight of stairs, littered with scraps of train and cinema tickets, the wall on the side smeared with red stains of betel leaf. The man opened the door on the right, and led him into a small room, modestly furnished with a desk and few chairs. The man behind the desk, a portly looking man in his forties was in the midst of a telephone conversation. He was dark, and nearly bald, with a few remnant strands of hair dangling precariously above his large ears. He had a large mole on his left cheek.

The young man left, closing the door behind him. Akhil Banerjee glanced around the room. The plaster was peeling off the walls. A few photographs, he assumed from the latest stage performances, hung on one of the side walls. Every inch of the desk in front was covered with scraps of paper, which had been restrained from flying off, by several paper weights. A dust covered ceiling fan droned above.

'What can I do for you?' asked the manager, replacing the receiver and motioning Akhil Banerjee to take a chair.

'Umm . . . *iye* . . . my name is Bhairav Ghosh,' started Akhil Banerjee, settling down on the nylon netted chair. 'I am a freelance writer. I am currently working on an article on the theatre culture of Calcutta. I was hoping to include Satyam Theatres . . . but of course, I don't want to impose. I understand if you are busy. . . .'

'*Arrey*, no, no Ghosh babu,' protested the manager. 'In the business of theatre, any publicity is good publicity. What do you say? Tea?'

'No, thank you,' said Akhil Banerjee.

'So tell me, what can I do for you, sir?'

Akhil Banerjee took out a notebook and a pen from his cloth bag, and opened a fresh page. He asked a few questions about the origin of Satyam Theatre, and the manager (whose name was Bibhash Kanti), launched into a lengthy and passionate narrative of his company's humble beginnings. Akhil Banerjee jotted everything down with utmost seriousness.

'Thank you, Kanti babu,' said Akhil Banerjee. 'I was wondering. . .' he hesitated.

'Tell me, Ghosh babu. . . .'

'Would it be possible to have a word with the rest of your production team? The actors, the helpers?'

'Why, yes of course! They are all upstairs rehearsing for *The Return of Layla Bibi*. Is anyone there?' he called out.

The young man, who had earlier escorted Akhil Banerjee to the manager's office, arrived.

'Take babu upstairs to the rehearsal room.'

Akhil Banerjee thanked Kanti babu profusely, and followed the man out of the office. Sound of loud raucous laughter reached their ears even before the door opened.

'It's a historical piece,' explained the man.

He led Akhil Banerjee into a large hall. The four men and two women, who were in the midst of a scene, stopped abruptly.

'Nomoshkar,' said Akhil Banerjee. 'I am a writer, researching for an article on theatres in Calcutta. Kanti babu said I could speak to you for a few minutes.'

'Okay,' they nodded.

Akhil Banerjee looked at the men carefully, without lingering too long on any one of them. He made a quick mental comparison with the image of Sujit he had in his mind. On the face of it, none of them seemed to fit the description. They were either too tall or too broad. Sujit had a lean thin structure, he remembered.

He asked each of them a question or two about life in the theatres. He listened carefully to the sound of their voices. He asked the women about the importance of their roles in the piece, said a quick thank you, and left.

On his way down, he peeped into Kanti babu's office and thanked him again for his help.

'Anytime, sir!' beamed the manager. 'Just drop in whenever you need information. And our next show will be in Uttam Mancha next Saturday. Please do come!'

★

'*Ei ki*? Where are you off to again?' asked Joyoti Bose. Bibhuti Bose strapped on his sandals and stood up.

'Um . . . I have to go out.'

'Going out? Where? You just returned!'

'I forgot to buy *paan*.'

'How many times have I told you to take my list? Is it possible to remember everything? Now just for paan you will have to go again in this heat. Remember to take the umbrella,' she hollered on the way to the kitchen.

Chandan Mukherjee, wearing yet another white dhuti-panjabi and puffing a Filter Wills, was already at the decided meeting point, when Bibhuti Bose arrived.

'How many *dhuti–panjabis* do you have, moshai?' asked Bibhuti Bose.

'Heh-heh,' laughed Chandan Mukherjee. 'I'm the quintessential Bengali babu. What do you say? Come let's take a taxi.'

They crossed the main road and waited for an empty cab to arrive.

'Where to?' asked a cab driver slowing down.

'Tollygunj.'

The driver shook his head and whizzed past.

'Did you look at that?' cried Bibhuti Bose. 'If they don't want to take passengers, why ask? Why drive around the city with a FOR HIRE sign?'

Chandan Mukherjee shook his head. 'If this was the West Bibhuti babu, we could have taken the driver to court. You see that traffic constable there, chewing tobacco and chasing off flies? You think he cares whether the people get a taxi or not. That's why these scoundrels don't give a damn. I shudder to think what will happen to this country in another ten or fifteen years.'

'Bunch of criminals, moshai.'

The second cab driver too, on hearing the destination, shook his head and drove off.

A third taxi arrived. 'Where to?' asked the driver in a gruff voice.

'Where do you want to go?' asked Bibhuti Bose.

The driver looked at him incredulously. 'Where do I want to go? You are the passenger babu . . . you tell me where you want to go.'

'You will not go where I want to go. So why don't you tell me where you want to go?'

The driver looked at the two of them, shook his head and drove off.

'I think we should try for an auto,' said Chandan Mukherjee.

The three-wheeled auto that arrived had three passengers at the back; Two boys in their late teens and a lady. The auto-driver indicated the two seats on his either side to Bibhuti Bose and Chandan Mukherjee.

'Are you mad?' asked Chandan Mukherjee. 'Are we teenagers that we will sit with our legs dangling outside like it was some kind of a joy ride?'

The two young boys from behind climbed out.

'You can take our seats, kaku,' they offered and settled themselves in the front.

'Thank you, bhai,' said Bibhuti Bose going in first. Chandan Mukherjee adjusted the folds of his *dhuti*, supported himself with his walking stick and climbed in with much effort.

The auto zigzagged its way through a maze of traffic. Bibhuti Bose hid his nostrils and mouth behind his elbow. 'Pollution,' he explained to Chandan Mukherjee, who held on to the metal rods for dear life.

'This is why I don't like autos, moshai,' said Bibhuti Bose as they got off at the Tollygunj Tram Depot. 'The polluting fumes, plus the noise. Uff! Horrible!'

They started walking towards the studio.

'What do we say when we get in, Bibhuti babu?' asked Chandan Mukherjee. 'We need to have some excuse for being there. Bibhuti babu, are you listening?'

Bibhuti Bose motioned him to stop talking. He was staring at something across the road, and indicated to Chandan Mukherjee to look in that direction. Chandan Mukherjee adjusted his spectacles, but could not see anything of significance.

'What is it, Bibhuti babu?' he whispered.

'Subhash.'

'Subhash? Who is Subhash?'

'*Arrey durr*, moshai . . . the one we are after! That Subhash!'

'Oh you mean Sujit? Where?'

'There . . . in front of the cigarette stall, wearing a blue half-shirt. Don't you see?'

Chandan Mukherjee squinted.

'Let's move closer, moshai. I can't be sure.'

They crossed the road and stood some distance away from the man in the blue shirt. They could now see his profile.

'Are you sure, Bibhuti babu?'

'Looks like him. Similar height, similar build . . . I am trying to imagine that face with a beard on. Chandan babu, wait here. Keep an eye on him. I'll be right back,' said Bibhuti Bose.

He returned presently with a copy of the *Anandabazaar Patrika*.

'*Ei ki* moshai, you want to read the paper now?' asked Chandan Mukherjee.

'*Arrey*, no, no, Chandan babu. Haven't you seen in the movies, when the detectives follow suspects, they always hide their faces behind the newspaper. Here, you take the sports section.'

Chandan Mukherjee, who needed to hold on to his walking-stick with one hand and the dangling end of his dhoti with the other, decided not to take the newspaper.

'Let us both read from the same paper, moshai,' he suggested.

'Have you seen the news of the Birbhum floods this year? Disastrous!' said Bibhuti Bose.

The jingling of bells announced the arrival of a tram.

'Every year it is the same, moshai. Yet the people are thoroughly unprepared. No organized evacuation plan.'

'Bibhuti babu, quick he is getting away! Get on to the tram. *Ei roko, roko*, stop!'

Since the tram was quite full, Bibhuti Bose and Chandan Mukherjee had to remain standing. Although they could not see Blue Shirt's face from where they were, they could make out that he was right at the front, just behind the driver's seat.

The ticket conductor approached them and thumbed the crisp notes neatly folded and held tightly between his knuckles. Bibhuti Bose paid for the two of them. As the tram lurched along, he craned his neck to catch a glimpse of Blue Shirt's face, and made eye-contact for a flickering second. Was there a hint of recognition in his eyes? Bibhuti Bose quickly buried his face under the newspaper.

At Gariahat, there was a sudden commotion. Gariahat, being the favourite market place of south Calcuttans, was teeming with last-minute Puja shoppers. Passengers, carrying bulky 'Big Shopper' bags elbowed their way into the tram, even before the ones inside could get off. A yelling ensued between those wanting to get in and those wanting to get out. Some yelled at the conductor who himself had been pushed out of the tram in the hustle. Just as the conductor managed to climb aboard and tug at the string (thus ringing the bell, announcing to the driver they were ready to start again) Bibhuti Bose yelled, '*Ei roko, roko,* we have to get down!' He motioned hastily at Chandan Mukherjee, who had just managed to find a seat and had settled down comfortably.

The conductor glared at Bibhuti Bose. '*Ki moshai*?' he yelled. 'Had you fallen asleep?'

Bibhuti Bose and Chandan Mukherjee got off hurriedly, and crossed over to the footpath.

'Where did he go, moshai?'

'Don't know. Can't see him anywhere,' replied Bibhuti Bose. They glanced up and down the footpath, either side of which was lined with makeshift stalls selling everything from bed sheets to dresses to lingerie. Hawkers screamed out their wares and announced the discounts of the day. The two walked towards the main crossing, craning their necks over the sea of people, hoping to catch a glimpse of Blue Shirt.

'Slippers! Slippers! Will you take babu?' yelled a hawker, dangling a pair in front of Bibhuti Bose's nose. 'Buy 1 get 1 free!!'

'*Arrey*, no, no.' Bibhuti Bose brushed him aside.

'I see him. I see him,' said Chandan Mukherjee, pointing up ahead. They quickened their pace. Pushing their way through the crowd was proving to be difficult as scores of people came from the opposite direction, slowing them down. Chandan Mukherjee found himself behind a lady clad in a red sari. The lady seemed deft at manoeuvring through the crowds, dodging here and ducking there in order to avoid getting hit by the oncoming shoppers who walked like zombies lost in the array of colourful wares displayed on either side of the sidewalk.

Bibhuti Bose spotted Blue Shirt a few paces ahead. As if sensing the doom that was catching up on him, Blue Shirt turned around. He caught sight of Bibhuti Bose screaming '*Pakro, pakro!*' (Catch him!)

Blue Shirt turned around and made a dash for the main road. The two pushed their way through the crowd. Blue Shirt had just reached the end of the footpath when the signal turned red. He shot back a glance, and was about to sprint across the main road when a strong pull brought him back on the pavement. A robust looking man, with bulging biceps held on to his shirt.

'Are you mad, dada?' he screamed, as a minibus honked loudly and breezed past, leaving behind a cloud of exhaust fumes. 'You would have been under that bus by now.'

Blue Shirt glanced behind his shoulders. The two gentlemen were panting already. He looked at the signal timer. Five seconds to go. . . .

'*Pakro*!' he heard someone scream behind him.

Three seconds . . . Two . . . Blue Shirt made a run for it.

For a second everything went black. Then he felt a pair of rough hands, pulling him up, and pinning him against the wall. It was the muscular man who had saved his life only a few seconds ago. What an irony! He thought. His forehead hurt. He could feel a trickle of warm blood. He could not see very clearly . . . everything was hazy. A crowd had gathered around him. They whispered 'pick-pocket, pick-pocket'.

'Police! Police!' That gentleman he had seen at Mr Agarwal's house was yelling excitedly.

A traffic constable arrived, thumbing tobacco in the cup of his palm.

'*Kya baat hain?*' (What's the matter?) asked the constable.

'This man, he is a criminal,' thundered Bibhuti Bose. 'Arrest him immediately!'

Blue Shirt/Sujit opened his mouth to speak, but the constable ordered him to shut up. A couple of police-men arrived. They handcuffed Sujit, and prodded him along. But somehow it was difficult to walk. Sujit took a step, but was about to trip and fall again. Something was stuck between his feet, preventing him from taking a step. He looked down.

'*Yeh kiska hain?*' (Whose is this?) asked the constable, bending down and freeing a walking stick that had entangled itself between Sujit's feet.

From behind the crowd, Chandan Mukherjee emerged with his arm outstretched.

'It's mine, it's mine,' he beamed.

A Confession

'Korta babu . . . phone,' said Kanai, as he handed the cordless receiver to Akhil Banerjee.

'Good afternoon, sir. I hope I am not disturbing you?'

'Arrey, Rakshit? No, no, not at all. Tell me.'

'Very good news, sir. Sujit has been caught!'

'Really? Congratulations! How? Where?'

'Don't congratulate me, sir. It was your friends Bibhuti Bose and Chandan Mukherjee. They chased him down Gariahat market and nabbed him with the help of some young men, I believe. I'm going down to the Gariahat police station myself. Would you like to come along, sir?'

'Yes, of course!'

'Very well, sir. I will pick you up in ten minutes.'

'Thank you, Rakshit.'

Sudarshan Rakshit arrived ten minutes later to find Akhil Banerjee waiting outside his house.

'Are Bibhuti babu and Chandan babu still there?' he asked as soon as he had climbed in.

'I believe so. I must say, they have put my entire police department to shame,' smiled Sudarshan Rakshit.

Akhil Banerjee tried to imagine his friends' faces when they would have caught Sujit. It made him smile too.

'What about Mr Agarwal? Has he been informed?'

'Yes I called him as soon as I heard the news of the capture. We will bring Sujit down to the Jadavpur Police Station later today. Mr Agarwal will be called to identify him of course.'

'Oh, by the way,' continued Sudarshan Rakshit, 'not that it matters anymore, but I did speak to the Bhawanipore Police station. . . .'

'Hmm . . . What did they say?'

'Well, it seems Mr Agarwal had stayed in Bhawanipore for almost twelve years and the police had been called only once, following the death of his wife.'

'Why is that?'

'Suicide. Seems she suffered from chronic depression. Took an overdose of sleeping pills.'

'Any suicide note?'

'No. But her brother produced letters that she had written to him, confirming that she was indeed suffering from severe depression and anxiety.'

'Hmm . . . I see.'

★

Debdas Guha Roy couldn't wait to get rid of his students. It had been an unusual morning thus far.

First – the phone call from Mr Ganguly. He had seen Piya's matrimonial advertisement, and would like to visit the Guha Roys the following month, right after Pujo. He had sounded genial, the voice was warm, full of an easy-going attitude that Debdas Guha Roy loved. The boy, Rajshekhar Ganguly was a cardiologist in Delhi's top heart hospital. Debdas Guha Roy had been smiling to himself throughout the conversation. Doctor Rajshekhar Ganguly! The name itself was enough to bring solace to heart patients. And to top it all, they were brahmins, and had no issues about an alliance with a kayastha family. Such broad-mindedness!

Even as Chhaya Guha Roy, scrutinized all the responses, her husband was content to sit back in his armchair, newspaper spread out in front of him, and gloat about his future son-in-law. A doctor! As far as he knew there were no doctors in their family thus far. There were plenty of engineers, and C.As, and professors . . . but no doctors. This would be a first. Perhaps Piya could do a nursing course. That way she could help out if they opened a nursing home in the future. Or maybe do a course in Hospital Management? That too was a very good option. He had heard about it from one of his students.

A telephone ring interrupted his reverie.

'Hello?' spoke Debdas Guha Roy into the receiver.

'Hello, Debdas babu?'

'Arrey Joj Saheb! Tell me. . . '

'Terrific news, moshai! Bibhuti babu and Chandan babu have caught Sujit! They're at the Gariahat Police Station. I'm going down there myself. Would you like to come too?'

'Umm . . . I cannot, Joj Saheb. I'm giving tuitions this afternoon.'

'Oh . . . no problem. See you later then. Bye.'

'Uh . . . Joj Saheb?'

'Yes, Debdas babu?'

'Are you leaving right now?'

'In about ten minutes. Rakshit will pick me up.'

'Oh, okay. I will call you later then.'

'Okay, bye.'

'Bye, Joj Saheb.'

Debdas Guha Roy replaced the receiver, hesitated for a second, then put on his sandals.

'Baba, are you going out?' asked Diya. 'Don't you have a class now?'

'Yes I know. I will be back soon. . .'

The doorbell rang. The sun burnt faces of Dhruba and Piyush greeted him, and Debdas Guha Roy decided that the matter at hand would have to wait for now.

After lecturing for a couple of hours, during which Debdas Guha Roy was unusually distracted, and seemed to lose his train of thought frequently, Dhruba and Piyush gathered their notebooks and left. Debdas Guha Roy quietly slipped on his sandals, and made for the door.

The doorbell rang again.

'Kaku, chanda,' announced Somen.

'O chanda? Listen I am in a hurry. Can you come back later? Maybe tomorrow?'

★

Akhil Banerjee and Sudarshan Rakshit were welcomed by an ecstatic Bibhuti Bose and Chandan Mukherjee.

'Moshai, if you are this swift with your arthritis, I wonder how you would be without,' laughed Akhil Banerjee as he hugged his friends. The thrill and pride that showed on their beaming faces only increased when Sudarshan Rakshit added, 'Hats off to you Mr Bose, Mr Mukherjee!', with a curt salute.

'So tell me, how did it all happen?' asked Akhil Banerjee, as they settled down on the chairs.

Bibhuti Bose and Chandan Mukherjee took turns to recount the events that had led to the capture of Sujit. Given their excited state of mind, they could well be forgiven for the few extra superlatives used in their narration.

Once the narration was over, Akhil Banerjee asked Saurav Biswas, the police inspector at the Gariahat Station whether he could meet Sujit once.

'Yes, of course. Please come with me, sir.'

He led the four of them to a cell with three inmates. Sujit sat in the far corner, legs drawn to his chest, his bandaged forehead hidden under his folded arms. From the way his shoulders trembled, it was evident he was sobbing.

'Sujit!' hollered Saurav Biswas, 'Come here! Joj Saheb wants to talk to you.'

He did not oblige. Saurav Biswas was about to yell again, but Akhil Banerjee stopped him. 'It's alright. Maybe another time.'

They thanked Mr Biswas and climbed on to Sudarshan Rakshit's jeep. 'We will be bringing him to Jadavpur later today. A day or two of questioning will reveal everything.'

The jeep meandered its way out of the Gariahat crossing and into Rash Behari Avenue.

'Oh, oh Mr Rakshit . . . could you please stop the jeep here for a minute?' said Bibhuti Bose. 'My slippers came apart during the chase. There was a hawker here, who was giving a good deal. . .'

The jeep pulled to a stop, and Bibhuti Bose got out.

'I'll only be a minute,' he said.

'*Ei* how much for that pair?' he asked the hawker who was still screaming the discount of the day.

'55 rupees, babu.'

'How much will you give it for?'

'50 rupees babu, not less than that.'

'Here take 40. Wrap it up. And also that pair,' said Bibhuti Bose pointing to another one in the row.

'That's another 50 rupees babu,' replied the hawker.

'What? You said Buy 1 Get One Free! I bought one pair, so the second pair should be free!'

'No, no . . . babu,' laughed the hawker. 'You misunderstood me . . . I meant buy 1 slipper and get its pair for free. . .'

'You thief, are you trying to fool me?!'

'Is there a problem, sir?' Sudarshan Rakshit appeared from behind.

'Arrey this man here. . .'

'Babu, babu! I was only joking . . . ha, ha. Just pulling your leg, that's all. Here, here take your second pair.' He quickly slipped a second new pair into a plastic bag, and handed it to Bibhuti Bose.

Bibhuti Bose took the bag, glared at the hawker for a brief second, and muttered a deadly word before turning away.

'Criminals!'

★

'I have a confession, Joj Saheb.'

Akhil Banerjee motioned him to a sofa, and sat down on one himself. Kanai went to fetch tea.

'Confession, Debdas babu?'

'Yes, well you see,' Debdas Guha Roy hesitated, 'that evening at Mr Agarwal's . . .'

'Yes?'

'Well, after Mr Agarwal showed us the ring, he put the box on the bookshelf in the living room, right? Some minutes later Mr Agarwal excused himself. Do you remember? Well . . . I don't know why I did it, but I wanted to take a second look at the ring. You see, as a geologist, rocks and stones have always fascinated me. I suppose you could call it curiosity, and I couldn't help myself. I really shouldn't have. I feel so stupid.'

'Please continue, Debdas babu.'

'Well, I went to see the thing one more time. Mr Agarwal was not in the room, and all of you were engrossed in conversation, so none of you paid any attention to me. I opened the box . . . and the ring was still there!'

'Hmm . . . then that must mean. . .'

'It wasn't Sujit! It couldn't have been. Sujit had left by then.'

'Hmm . . . this is very interesting. What did you do?'

'Well nothing really. I quickly closed the lid and came back to join the conversation.'

'Why did you not mention this before, Debdas babu?'

'Please forgive me, Joj Saheb. I did not want to draw attention to it as I was very embarrassed by my own act. I mean, what would Mr Agarwal think? Actually I thought I could get away with my secret . . . but now that Sujit has been caught . . . after all it's a question of a man's entire life. I couldn't possibly stay silent any longer, Joj Saheb. I hope you are not angry with me. I was merely. . .'

'Arrey no no, Debdas babu. You did the right thing by telling me. In fact, this is a vital piece of information you have given me. If it had not been for your curiosity, Sujit would have had to spend a few years behind the bars.'

'I hope he will be set free now.'

'Hmm . . . I suppose so. . .'

'Will I get into trouble, Joj Saheb?'

'No no, relax Debdas babu. Nothing will happen to you.'

'Uff, I feel so relieved now! Ever since that evening, this has been eating me up inside. Everyone was pointing fingers at that poor fellow, but I knew it couldn't be him.'

Debdas Guha Roy finished his tea and got up to leave.

'By the way, Debdas babu, in your opinion, how much do you think a diamond like that is worth? I am referring to the intrinsic value of course.'

'See Joj Saheb, that is another thing that has been bothering me,' Debdas Guha Roy hesitated.

'What do you mean?'

'You see, I have a feeling . . . that the stone is not a diamond at all.'

'Not diamond!'

'No, my best guess is cubic zirconia. It is available in jewellery shops everywhere. It is used as a diamond substitute. But of course I saw the thing only for a few seconds, I could be wrong. I am sure Mr Agarwal, being a seasoned collector would know the difference.'

Akhil Banerjee's face turned serious.

'You may be more right than you think you are, Debdas babu,' he said slowly, his brows knitted in deep thought. 'I for one know that Van Gogh's grave is not in Paris. It is in a small village called Auverse, north-west of Paris. I know, because I have been there myself.'

Durga Pujo: Then and Now

'Oh ho! What's the matter Chandan babu? I see you are not in your *dhuti-panjabi* today?' smiled Debdas Guha Roy as he approached the park. Chandan Mukherjee, dressed in a half-shirt, and trousers was doing forward bends.

'Ha, ha . . . the thing is Debdas babu, *dhuti-panjabi* is fine . . . but one can't really exercise in it.'

'Moshai, I can't stay without congratulating you and Bibhuti babu! My god! What a show! How did you. . . ?'

'Ah! Here comes Bibhuti babu!'

'I was just telling Chandan babu,' said Debdas Guha Roy to Bibhuti Bose as he neared the duo. 'You two deserve a medal, moshai!'

Bibhuti Bose laughed.

'Come join us for a walk, Bibhuti babu,' said Debdas Guha Roy.

'How come I don't see Joj Saheb, today?' asked Bibhuti Bose. The three of them walked along the perimeter. Every now and then Chandan Mukherjee stretched out his arms and yelled 'HA!'

'It's good for the lungs,' he explained to his friends.

The morning air was crisp. It had that familiar 'Pujo feeling' . . . one that Bengalis knew all too well, but could never explain. The sky was the purest blue, painted in parts by the fleeting white cotton-like clouds that seemed to be the forbearers of the festival that was only a few days away.

'I hear the club house is available these days?' asked Debdas Guha Roy.

'You are right. These days those buggers are busy with the Pujo decorations. By the way, have you seen our *pandal* this year? What do they think they are doing, moshai? With fountains and chandeliers, how much do you think it would have cost?'

'Quite a lot I'm sure. The purpose of Pujo nowadays is no longer to make Ma Durga happy,' said Chandan Mukherjee. 'Each club will try to outdo the other by spending lavishly on *pandal* decorations and lighting. Ask any one of these organisers the first line of Pujo mantra and you'll see. . .' he sighed.

'You are right, Chandan babu,' said Debdas Guha Roy. 'I remember when I was young, how eagerly I would wait for Panchami. The idol for our Pujo at Charu Avenue was brought in every year on the day of Panchami, and my mother along with the other ladies of the neighbourhood would spend the whole day adorning her with sari and jewellery. Ma Durga was coming to stay in the home of her parents, my mother used to tell us. It was very important to welcome her with love and warmth, so that she came back every year. . .'

'Hmm . . . The face of Durga Pujo in Calcutta has changed so much,' said Bibhuti Bose. 'During our childhood, most of the *pujo*s used to be in the homes of the rich . . . Sovabazaar palace, Mullickbari . . . these type of *sarbojonin pujas* were rare, and not at all sought after. We would prefer to go to family-run *pujas* . . . the *pujo* would be done with so much devotion and the food used to be so delicious!'

'I remember I saw my first bull-slaughter in Sovabazaar,' said Chandan Mukherjee. 'I was barely eight . . . My god! Some friends told me that there was going to be a bull-slaughter at the Rajbari. We decided to go. But the *durwan*, the gatekeeper, was letting in only friends and relatives of the family, and not allowing anyone else in. Some men were trying to get in, and the durwan kept pushing them away. Somehow in that commotion we slipped in. The anticipation and the thrill that throbbed with every breath . . . I can still see the scene clearly in front of my eyes . . . These days Pujo is a circus,' he said, pointing to the hoarding at the entry of Uday Shankar Sarani – *Come see Ma Durga and her children. They come to Sabuj Kalyan riding on live animals this year!* He shook his head.

'Whatever you say, Chandan babu,' said Debdas Guha Roy, 'It's somehow difficult to believe that the victory celebration of the Battle of Plassey, or Polashir Juddho as we Bengalis like to call it, has now become the national identity for all Bengalis.'

'What do you mean, Debdas babu?' asked Chandan Mukherjee. 'What has the Battle of Plassey got to do with Durga Pujo?'

'It's quite interesting, really. Just the other day I was reading a book by Radharaman Roy. He says, that Nabakrishna Deb, who we all know as the founder of the Sovabazar dynasty, was actually a *munshi*, a clerk in the East India Company. In those days, Bengal was under the rule of the Nawabs. Hence all official work used to be in Persian. Now these munshis acted as interpreters and translators between the Nawabs and the East India Company. Nabakrishna was also a private tutor to Warren Hastings, he would teach him Persian.

'Now, on 23 June 1757, Nawab Siraj-ud-Daula was defeated at the hands of Robert Clive in the Battle of Plassey. Even though this was in fact an important victory for the East India Company, Nabakrishna Deb and his counterpart, Krishnachandra Roy of Nadia, interpreted this as a victory of Hindus over Muslims. Robert Clive, being the shrewd statesman that he was, actually supported this idea, and believe it or not, it was Clive who suggested to Nabakrishna Deb that this victory be celebrated by performing a Hindu Puja. Can you imagine?! Clive was a Christian and strongly opposed idol worship, but simply for the sake of politics, he encouraged Nabakrishna Deb to organize a Durga Pujo.

'Earlier Durga Pujo used to be celebrated in parts of Bengal only during the spring time, and the Nabapatrika Pujo in autumn. Now, Nabakrishna decided to shift the timing of the Durga Pujo, and celebrated it in the autumn month. So the first autumnal Durga Pujo actually took place in the year 1757, as a victory celebration of the Battle of Plassey. The Nabaptrika Pujo and the Durga Pujo got intermingled with one another. In the following years, he encouraged more and more zamindars to do the same. When the 'babus' of Bengal saw that this Pujo had the blessings of the East India Company, they fell over each other to please the sahibs, inviting them over, feeding them beef and foreign liquor, even arranging for *baiji's* to come from all over the country to entertain them. I would say, in that respect *pujo*s these days are far more *sattvik*. Don't you think?'

Chandan Mukherjee shook his head. 'I can't believe it, Debdas babu. Durga Pujo was performed by Lord Rama before his epic journey to slay the demon Ravana. Isn't it? And he did this *pujo* in autumn. That is why we also perform Durga Pujo in autumn. Isn't it?'

'Well, according to Radharaman Roy, there is no historical evidence to support this fact. The autumnal worship of Ma Durga by Lord Rama is found only in Krittibas's *Ramayana* and not in Balmiki's *Ramayana*. It could well have been the poet's imagination.'

'No, moshai, I cannot agree,' Chandan Mukherjee shook his head.

'Moshai, I have always wondered,' said Bibhuti Bose, 'how come of all the gods and goddesses in India, it is Ma Durga that we worship with such devotion in Bengal? I mean Lord Rama was from the North, and he went to Lanka from the South, crossing the Indian Ocean. Where does Bengal come into the picture?'

'Bibhuti babu, you have raised an interesting point,' said Debdas Guha Roy. 'Durga Pujo in Bengal has nothing much, or very little, to do with Lord Rama. You see, agriculture and farming have always been the main occupations of rural Bengal. And in the olden days it was the womenfolk who used to take care of much of the farming. Their position in society was higher than that of men. Hence one sees a predominance of goddesses rather than gods in Bengal – Durga, Lakshmi, Saraswati. . . .

'Now the main enemy of the farmers in those days was the wild buffalo. Hence an idol was created depicting a female goddess capturing and taming a wild buffalo. She was called Mahish-mordini, killer of buffalo. Later when society became dominated by men, the buffalo was replaced by a half-man and half-bull image, depicting the thwarting of both by a woman.'

'Debdas babu, are you saying that all the mythological stories we have heard since childhood are false?'

'Moshai, a mythological story is just that . . . a story. When one goes into the history of how certain cultures and traditions came into being, one can understand many of the practices. If you go to the Indian Museum you will see an old idol of Ma Durga, probably belonging to the 2nd century. It shows the goddess with two hands only, and with one hand she is holding on to the tail of a buffalo. The oldest idol of Mahishasurmardini, the killer of the demon Mahishasura dates back to the 10th century.'

They walked on in silence for a while, reflecting on what they had just heard.

'Do you remember the *jalsas*, moshai?' asked Bibhuti Bose. 'Manna Dey, Hemonto, Haimonti Shukla . . . ah ha . . . to listen to their songs in that informal, homely atmosphere!'

'*Nil akasher nichey prithibi . . . Aar prithibir uporey oi nil akash, tumi dekhecho ki*? 'He hummed a couple of lines of a Bengali song of yesteryears.

'Those days are gone, Bibhuti babu. Now Ma Durga has to be content listening to Bollywood! I hear this year Biplab has cancelled the theatre as well. Diya told me they said they don't have funds for it. Such a tragedy!' Debdas Guha Roy shook his head.

'Is Bubai coming this year for Pujo, Chandan babu?' asked Bibhuti Bose.

'He has been here since last week. Though I haven't seen his face for a while.'

'Hmm. . .'

'God knows what he does, locked up in his room. . .' continued Chandan Mukherjee. 'Sometimes I think he has fallen into bad company . . . what if he is taking drugs . . .?'

'Arrey, no no, Chandan babu!' protested Debdas Guha Roy. 'A brilliant boy like Bubai? I cannot believe it! He stood 3rd in the Higher Secondary exams, 12th in the IIT entrance test. No one from our *paara* has come anywhere near that!'

'Yes true . . . but still. You know young boys of today . . . they get influenced so easily . . . One never knows. . .'

★

Akhil Banerjee walked out of the Jadavpur Police Station into the blazing sun. He shaded his eyes, and glanced up and down the street to locate Balram, his driver.

'Saab, here!' called out Balram, waving his arms.

Akhil Banerjee crossed the street, got into his car. 'Ballygunj,' he told Balram.

He recalled his conversation with Sudarshan Rakshit. Mr Agarwal had identified Sujit to be the very same man who had visited him on the evening of the party. Sujit was being questioned thoroughly, but he was not cooperating at all. He claimed he was innocent. Over and over again. That is all he would ever say.

The ambassador meandered through the busy Dhakuria Bridge, circled Golpark, and made its way to Gariahat. The streets were jammed with cars, buses and auto-rickshaws, all honking, yelling at each other to give an inch of space to move forward. The pavements were chock-a-block with Puja shoppers. As Akhil Banerjee's car waited at the signal, a young boy approached him. His naked, frail body was smeared with dust and dirt. He held a plate in one hand, in which was placed a photo of an idol, a flower and a few coins. With his right hand he mimicked putting food in his mouth. Balram shouted at him. The boy fled. The signal changed and the car moved forward.

When they arrived at Ballygunj, Akhil Banerjee asked Balram to take him to Sharma Sweets.

'It will be impossible to find parking here, sir. Let me drop you here, and I will come back to fetch you in fifteen minutes.'

'Very good,' said Akhil Banerjee.

He got off the car and walked over to Sharma Sweets. The shop was crowded and it took Akhil Banerjee several minutes to get to the counter. His order of sweets packed and paid for, he stepped out of the shop and shaded his eyes to locate his car.

On his way back, he asked Balram to look out for the beggar boy. Just as they had reached Golpark, he saw the boy begging at the window of another car.

'*Ei* . . . come here!' called out Akhil Banerjee.

The boy hesitated . . . Akhil Banerjee showed him a packet of sweets. The boy ran towards him, grabbed the packet and darted to the pavement. In the seconds before the signal changed to green, several other children had gathered around the boy, and a fight for a morsel had broken out.

★

Poltu took a final look at the mirror and ran his finger through his hair. This was the moment he had been waiting for. It was a matter of sheer good luck that yesterday, when he had accompanied the boys to Piya's house for chanda collection, her father had been in a hurry and had not obliged. The boys had cursed of course, but Poltu had been thankful. He wasn't really prepared that day. He had been pushed to the back by the likes of Partho and Somen, and had had to stand on tiptoe and crane his neck for a glimpse of Piya. Good thing Piya hadn't answered the door too. Was that how one met one's future bride and would-be father-in-law? With a gang of boys asking for money?

But today was Poltu's golden chance. He had somehow been able to convince Partho that he would take care of Haripada Das Lane. He would have liked to say, one particular house in Haripada Das Lane, but that would have made Partho and the others suspicious. Poltu did not mind the extra work, as long as it gave him a chance to speak to Piya. He hoped fervently that it would be she, who would answer the door today.

Partho had protested at first, given him sceptical looks, even challenged his sincerity. But Poltu had been adamant.

'I promise I won't let you down, Partho,' he had pleaded.

He rehearsed the scene several times in his mind. He would walk up to her door confidently, introduce himself, and ask for the *chanda* amount. If all went well thus far, he would ask Piya to go out with him.

Poltu brushed invisible dust from his shirt, smelled his armpit one last time, muttered Ma Kali's name and embarked on his mission.

Once in front of Piya's house, however, his footstep faltered. He felt an uneasy churning in his stomach, and his heart thumped wildly against his ribcage. He turned back. But then, he heard himself say, an opportunity like this might never come again. This could be the day that his life, and unknown to Piya, her's too, could change forever.

Poltu made up his mind. He couldn't let the boys down, but more importantly, he couldn't let himself down. He would go up to Piya's door and ring her doorbell, even if it meant immediate hospitalization.

He hesitantly opened the green gate and entered a small courtyard, on either side of which several flower pots had been neatly arranged. But Poltu had no time for nature appreciation at the moment. He took a deep breath, and rang the doorbell. When he heard footsteps behind the door, he wanted to flee. He turned around, but it was too late. The door had opened – the wooden door, not the iron collapsible gate that lay as an extra layer of security to keep away unwanted visitors.

'Who are you?' bellowed Debdas Guha Roy between the gaps of the collapsible gate.

'*Bah . . . ha . . .* '

'Who?'

'Po . . . ho . . . ho . . . nirban.'

'Pohonirban?'

Poltu shook his head vigorously. What he had really wanted to say was his formal name, Anirban. But given that he rarely had had the opportunity to use it, he had begun to blurt out his pet-name, and somewhere along the way decided to suffix it with his formal name.

'A . . . a . . . nirban.'

'Oh, Anirban. What do you want?'

'*Bah . . . ha . . . ha*'

'What?'

'*Cha ha . . . ha . . .* '

'*Cha*? Tea?'

Poltu shook his head.

'*Cha ha . . . haa*'

Debdas Guha Roy looked at him with mild irritation.

'*Cha . . . a . . . ha* . . . nda.' He managed finally.

'*Chanda*? *Pujo chanda*? Which club?'

'So . . . ho . . . buj . . . Ko . . . ho . . . lyan.'

'Sobuj Kalyan? Why would I give you *chanda*? I have never even seen you before! Where are Partho and Somen? Ask them to come if they want *chanda*.'

With those words, the wooden door slammed shut.

Poltu stared at the door. He had wanted to enquire about Piya. Was she home? Was she well? Simple words of love and concern with which he had hoped to convey his feelings. But somehow he knew, the wall, the wooden door and the iron collapsible gate that separated him from his love, were too thick to let in his feelings.

★

Akhil Banerjee sat on the reclining chair in his balcony. A myriad of thoughts raced through his mind.

It could not be this complicated, he told himself. It was simple, very simple . . . but what was he missing?

The light outside was beginning to fade, bringing with it the cawing of crows returning home. The sky had turned a dark crimson, the air smelt of *shiuli* flowers – that heady fragrance that always reminded one of Bengal, and of the arrival of Ma Durga. Bright halogen lights had been put up at the Sabuj Kalyan Park so that labourers could work late into the night. The clamour of their incessant hammering accompanied by the clattering of long bamboo sticks was signal enough that Durga Pujo was only a few days away. From the framework that had been put up so far, one could gather that the *pandal* was at least double the size of previous years. Had they brought in the idols already? He wondered.

He did not get up to switch on the light. He sat there for long, in the dark, thinking over the questions that bothered him. Presently he got up and made his way to the living room downstairs. From under a side table, he pulled out the telephone directory. A quick search provided him the number he was looking for.

★

Bikash had just paid the *auto-wallah* and turned towards Haripada Das Lane, when he almost collided with Akhil Banerjee.

'*Arrey* Sir, please pardon me. I didn't. . .'

'It's all right, Bikash babu,' Akhil Banerjee hastened to reassure him. 'If you don't mind, can I speak to you for a few minutes?'

'Me?' Bikash looked surprised.

'Ah, yes. It will only take a few minutes. Come let's stand under that tree, it's less hot over there.'

Bikash followed obediently, an enquiring look on his longish face.

'Bikash babu,' continued Akhil Banerjee, once they were comfortably under the tree shade, 'how long have you been working with Mr Agarwal?'

'About five years now. Ever since he moved here.'

'And before that he had another secretary, isn't it?'

'Yes. Sibu Burman.'

'Do you know why he left? Had Mr Agarwal mentioned anything in this connection?'

'Well, all I know is that he had left quite suddenly. Apparently he did not even give any notice to Mr Agarwal. He was of course very angry about the whole thing. I believe this was just a few days after the tragic death of Mrs Agarwal. The whole episode had left Mr Agarwal quite shocked and upset. When I took up this job, Mr Agarwal insisted that I give at least two months' notice if I wanted to leave.'

'Yes, yes, I understand. Have you ever met Sibu Burman? Did he ever come to this house?'

'No, never.'

'Does Mr Agarwal have any enemies? Anyone that would want to harm him?'

Bikash gulped and shook his head.

'I see you have done quite a bit of shopping, Bikash babu?' said Akhil Banerjee, indicating the three Big Shopper bags. Bikash smiled humbly and shrugged.

'*Oi* . . . nothing much really . . . heh heh,' he said.

'Does he pay you well?'

'Mr Agarwal, you mean?'

'I think you know who I mean, Bikash babu.'

Bikash's face turned pale and he gulped hard.

'I . . . I don't understand sir. . .' he muttered.

'On the contrary, I think you understand very well. Now please listen to what I have to tell you, or else you will get into deep trouble.'

What Really Happened

Mr Agarwal's living room was packed with people, but there was a distinct air of coldness in it, that somehow had nothing to do with the weather. Everyone was present including Sujit (now stripped off his beard and moustache) behind whose chair stood a police constable. In addition there was Bikash Bakshi, Sudarshan Rakshit, and another gentleman in his late fifties, dressed in an off-white safari suit, who sat silently in one corner. He had a square pockmarked face with thick eyebrows, and a balding head. He did not seem to recognize any of the people in the room, and kept staring at his hands or at the ceiling.

Mr Agarwal himself was seated on an armchair. His face bore a defeated look.

'What's the point, Juj Saab?' he asked. 'He will never confess. The ring is gone.' He sighed.

Akhil Banerjee stood up from his chair. All eyes followed him as he paced the living room.

'There is a point, Mr Agarwal and I will come to it presently,' he said. 'First let me quickly recapitulate the key events of the party and the subsequent few weeks.'

He stopped his walk and looked at every one of those present.

'On the evening of 7 July, Mr Agarwal invited a few gentlemen from our neighbourhood to his house. That included me, Bibhuti babu, Debdas babu, Chandan babu and Dr Mullick. We were all sitting here (he indicated the living room), talking. Then Mr Agarwal had a visitor. Sujit Hazra, who had earlier taken an appointment with him for this very time, came to sell some curio items. Mr Agarwal claimed that the items were bogus, and showed us a genuine historical piece from his collection; A diamond ring worth lakhs, which supposedly belonged to a late queen. Then Sujit Hazra said he had to leave. In his hurry he tripped and fell. One of us, namely Bibhuti babu helped him collect the things that had spilled out from his side bag. Sujit collected his things and left. Mr Agarwal in the meantime took the velvet box, and placed it on the bookshelf, there.' He pointed.

'The rest of us hung around for a while, and then we too took Mr Agarwal's leave. Now, Mr Agarwal claims that he stayed in the room for a while, and then decided to call it a day. He thought of taking a look at the ring again before putting it in his safe but found the box empty. He immediately notified the police. The servants were questioned, nothing was found.

'Naturally, all suspicion fell on Sujit Hazra, the one person who was a complete stranger to everyone here and the only one who looked like he was in need of money. Sujit could well be spending a few years in jail now, had it not been for a bit of curiosity on the part of our friend, Debdas Guha Roy. After Sujit had left, he had gotten up once more to see the ring. And it was still in the box!'

There was a collective gasp in the room. Sujit looked up from the floor for the first time.

'That must mean. . .' started Chandan Mukherjee.

'It wasn't Sujit,' finished Akhil Banerjee.

'What are you saying, Juj Saab?' asked Mr Agarwal. 'If not him, then who?'

Akhil Banerjee ignored his question and went on.

'The interesting point is that Mr Agarwal himself knew that it was not Sujit! Am I right?' He looked directly at Mr Agarwal whose face had turned red.

'What rubbish are you saying? How could I have known?'

'Joj Saheb, I'm really confused here,' said Chandan Mukherjee. 'Who has the ring?'

'Me. I have it.'

'What??? You?' Everyone looked at him aghast.

'I mean I have it now. But all this while, it was right here, in Mr Agarwal's house. The ring was never stolen.'

Several people spoke all at once. Mr Agarwal looked as shocked as the others. Questions were being hurled at Akhil Banerjee from all sides. He motioned them to stop.

'Please allow me to explain,' Akhil Banerjee continued calmly. 'After the incident, I asked Mr Agarwal if I could see his living room once more to which he had readily agreed. I reconstructed the scene exactly as it had happened, right up to the point where Sujit fell, picked up his belongings and left. And it became immediately clear that Sujit could not have had the opportunity to take the ring with all of us right there. Of course, this would have been difficult to prove without Debdas babu's confession. In fact, looking back I was sure that none of us had the opportunity to pick up the ring, without getting noticed. Now then, the puzzling question was why did Mr Agarwal insist that it was stolen?

'Let us forget about the ring for a second. Let us try and reconstruct an episode of Mr Agarwal's life. This happened say, six years ago. Mr Agarwal was then living in Bhowanipur with his wife. Mrs Agarwal was known to suffer from anxiety, paranoia and depression. She wrote several letters to her brother, insisting that someone, namely her husband, was trying to kill her.'

'Liar!' shot back Mr Agarwal.

'Please let me complete,' said Akhil Banerjee sternly. 'She may have also indicated that as she was the heiress to a large fortune, her husband, Mr Agarwal wanted her to give all her property to him.

'Like I said, this is only a reconstruction, a hypothesis. Now, after several such letters, one day Mrs Agarwal's brother receives the news of her death. The police claim it was a suicide, an overdose of sleeping pills. Her brother immediately comes to Calcutta, and discovers upon arrival that all her property, including a ring, a family heirloom, has been willed to her husband, Mr Agarwal.

'Her brother gets suspicious. He produces the letters his sister wrote to him, that said clearly that she was scared of her husband. The police dismiss it as a case of paranoia. Am I right, Mr Srivastav?'

The gentleman in the safari-suit looked up. He waited several seconds before answering.

'Mohan and I use to run a curio shop in New Delhi,' he said. His voice was hoarse, almost as if it took him a lot of effort to speak. 'He used to come to our house often, and was treated like family. One day, he said he wanted to marry my sister. I was so happy . . . we all were. They married and moved to Calcutta. But it was not in her destiny to be happy.

'She was extremely depressed with him. She wrote to me repeatedly, saying that he was asking her to sign a will. She was scared that if she did not give in to his demands, he would kill her. She was even scared to talk on the phone when I called her.

'Then one day, it all changed. She sounded really happy and relieved when I called her. She said she had signed a will, in which she had left her share of the family property to her husband. All, except the ring. That alone was worth lakhs. But more than the money, it has a very sentimental value for us. She told me explicitly over the phone, that the ring she would never leave to him. It was a family heirloom.

'Anyway, to be honest I was relieved too. The important thing was that she was happy again. She talked about going on a vacation to Nainital with her husband. Then just a week later, I heard the terrible news. She had committed suicide!' Mr Srivastav hid his face in the palms of his hands.

'I could not believe it, Juj Saab. It was impossible. I produced the letters to the police. They wouldn't hear anything of it. Your sister was prone to depression and suicidal thoughts, they asserted. It was useless. I told Mohan to at least return the ring, just as a memory keepsake, but he refused. He claimed that my sister had willingly left him everything, including the ring. I argued with him for days, but he just wouldn't budge. Even now, I sometimes call him up to see if he will change his mind. And every time he refuses, threatens to inform the police that I'm harassing him.'

'Rubbish! He is a liar!' thundered Mr Agarwal.

'Coming back to the death of Mrs Agarwal,' continued Akhil Banerjee. 'What if it really was a murder and not a case of suicide? Again this is only a hypothesis. Let us suppose that Mr Agarwal did coerce his wife to leaving everything to him in her will, and then seizing an opportunity, mixes the sleeping pills in her milk. The murder happens smoothly, and no one ever suspects Mr Agarwal. But . . . what if, there was a witness?

'Someone could have seen him stirring the milk, and later when the death was discovered, that someone, could have put two and two together and deduced that Mr Agarwal was a murderer. The people living in that house at the time were three servants, and a secretary Sibu Burman. The three servants continue to be in Mr Agarwal's employment, but his secretary disappears. It could be possible then that Sibu Burman, having been a witness to the murder, had decided to blackmail his boss. Mr Agarwal pays him a hefty amount and asks him to leave for good. Sibu Burman is only too happy that his plan has worked. He takes the money and leaves.

'Now, a few years later Sibu Burman is again in need of money. He considers contacting Mr Agarwal again, but by this time, unknown to him, his former boss has moved to a different locality. Sibu Burman takes up a small-time job at a local TV production studio.'

'Sujit?!' cried Chandan Mukherjee.

'Exactly.'

'So let's say that Sibu/Sujit is working nearby at Tollygunj Technician's studio. And one day, by sheer luck he spots Mr Agarwal on the street. He follows him back to his home. Finding out the phone number is easy enough. He calls up Mr Agarwal, on the pretext of showing him some rare curio items. Since Bikash Bakshi, his secretary is away on an errand, it was Mr Agarwal who answered the phone. He gives an appointment for Sunday evening, but later something strikes him about the caller. He may have recognized the caller's voice. He wonders if Sibu is back in town to harass him again.

'He quickly decides to organize a party and invite some of us at the very same time as Sujit Hazra/Sibu Burman's appointment. Surely, when Sibu sees that Mr Agarwal is friendly with a High Court Judge, he will know better than to bother him again.'

'You mean . . . we were all invited to scare away a blackmailer?' asked Debdas Guha Roy.

'Yes, precisely,' nodded Akhil Banerjee. 'Now, coming back to the events on the evening of the party . . . when Mr Agarwal recognizes Sujit as Sibu Burman, his previous secretary, he hatches a brilliant plan! He tells the police that a diamond ring, the very ring that he had shown his guests in front of Sujit/Sibu, has gone missing. Two immediate things are ensured. One, Sibu Hazra emerges as the prime suspect. So now, Sibu, already cautious that Mr Agarwal has friends in high places, will now surely not have the guts to bother him again.

'And two, Mr Srivastav, Mr Agarwal's brother-in-law, who often called from Kanpur to demand that he return the ring to him, now knowing for sure that the ring is stolen, will not bother Mr Agarwal again, thus killing two birds with one stone.

'It may not have been possible to catch Sibu/Sujit, had it not been for a brilliant suggestion by Chandan babu. Following this, we, the four of us, decided to visit different theatres and TV production companies in the area. Of course, as we all know now, it was squarely due to the heroic efforts of Bibhuti babu and Chandan babu that we were able to nab Sibu.

'Another suspicion of mine was later confirmed by Debdas babu. The ring that was shown to us was not worth lakhs of rupees as claimed by Mr Agarwal. It was in fact, an imitation, a fake.'

'What!' cried Mr Agarwal. 'Have you gone mad, Juj Saab? You have been hatching one fantastic story after another, one hypothesis after another, without an iota of proof! And now you say that the ring is a fake?! Show it to me!' he thundered. 'Let us all see the ring.'

Akhil Banerjee obliged. He took out a crumpled piece of paper from his pocket, and opened it carefully to reveal the ring. There was a stunned silence. The diamond ring, the one that had been shown on the evening of the party, lay there.

'Take a look Mr Agarwal,' said Akhil Banerjee. 'Do you think this is a genuine diamond?'

Mr Agarwal took the ring under the lamp. He pushed his spectacles over his head and brought the ring closer to his eyes. He inspected it for a long time, turning it this way and that.

'I don't understand,' he said finally. 'The stone. . .'

'It's an imitation, Mr Agarwal,' said Akhil Banerjee. 'The real one was stolen from you only a few days ago. And in its place a fake stone was placed.'

'But how? Who. . .?'

'Your brother-in-law, Pankaj Srivastav, had tried many different tactics to retrieve the ring. One of them was bribing your employee, Bikash Bakshi.'

'Bikash?'

'Yes. Mr Srivastav regularly paid Bikash babu good money to keep an eye on you. I suppose he had been asked to search for any incriminating evidence he could gather against you, and if he ever had the opportunity, to grab the ring and pass it on to Mr Srivastav. That opportunity presented itself a few days preceding the party. Mr Bikash Bakshi had replaced the original diamond with a fake one, and was ready to travel to Kanpur to hand over the stone.

'Unfortunately for him, the events that followed, prevented him from travelling anywhere under police orders. Bikash Bakshi had no choice but to lie low, and whenever possible call up Mr Srivastav in Kanpur to update him of the situation.'

Bikash Bakshi fidgeted nervously with the buttons of his shirt. Sudarshan Rakshit took the ring from Mr Agarwal.

'So the ring was a fake?' said Chandan Mukherjee more to himself than to anyone else. It seemed incredible to him that he had raced down Rash Behari Avenue to nab the wrong guy, falsely accused of stealing a fake ring.

'Yes, Chandan babu, it was. Just like that Jamini Roy on the wall, and perhaps like many other items on display here.'

'But then . . . where is the original ring? It must still be with Bikash Bakshi?' asked Dr Mullick.

'It was. He handed it over to the police last night,' replied Akhil Banerjee.

'Do you have anything to say, Mr Agarwal?' asked Sudarshan Rakshit.

'Liars!' bellowed Mr Agarwal. 'Get out of my house this minute!' he screamed.

'Mr Agarwal, Sibu has confessed to everything,' said Sudarshan Rakshit calmly.

He motioned to the constable, who approached Mr Agarwal to handcuff him. Mr Agarwal flung his arms about, but was soon restrained by the constable with some help from Rakshit.

'We are starting an enquiry into the death of your wife, Mr Agarwal,' said Sudarshan Rakshit. 'Please come to the police station with us.'

★

'*Baap re*, Joj Saheb! You are even more sensational than the detectives in the books!' cried Debdas, as soon as the police had left the room with Mr Agarwal.

'Criminal! Criminal! I always knew,' said Bibhuti Bose.

Pankaj Srivastav approached the four of them, his palms folded. 'I do not know how to thank you gentlemen. Please accept my deepest gratitude. . .'

'It's alright, Mr Srivastav,' said Akhil Banerjee patting his back. 'It's alright.'

They came out of Mr Agarwal's house. It was a clear night. There was a slight chill in the air. A carpet of *shiuli* flowers, wet with dew, lay under their feet. Several excited children had gathered around a lorry that had just rolled into Uday Shankar Sarani. Others came running, calling out to their friends. Ma Durga had arrived.

Tomorrow is Shashthi.

A Pujo Like No Other

Scores of people had gathered at the Sabuj Kalyan Park. The scene was almost exactly as Biplab Maity had imagined it would be. The children squealed excitedly, pointing at the swans and peacocks (well, two swans and one peacock to be precise) that ambled aimlessly in the garden. A gigantic fountain in the centre spluttered sporadic jets of water (a steady stream that would flow uninterruptedly from the top, could not be procured, given the state of the municipal corporation's water supply). The *pandal*, the abode of the goddess, stood towering above their heads, its complex bamboo structure delicately draped with yards of colourful cotton, its cornices done with intricate terra cotta patterns. From the ceiling hung a magnificent chandelier, one that Biplab had himself handpicked from the dozens that were available.

Goddess Durga, with her four children, adorned from head to foot in fake gold ornaments, occupied the stage. Ma Durga, with ten weapons in her ten arms, rage in her eyes, riding on a mighty clay lion, her spear piercing through the half-bull and half-man demon, Mahishasura. On her left – Saraswati, the goddess of knowledge, sat daintily on her swan, and Kartik, the bold warrior rode on his peacock. On her right were Lakshmi, the goddess of wealth with her owl, and Ganesh, the elephant-god with his mouse. The four children of Ma Durga looked beautiful in their costumes, a serene expression on their faces, oblivious of the demon their mother was trying to kill.

But the piece de resistance, the crowd-puller, was the magnificent lion that paraded restlessly in his cage. Magnificent was perhaps not the apt word. If truth be told, the lion was skinny and weak, and had aged considerably. It was tired, and perhaps even a little disgusted. It slept most of the time, and got up only when hungry.

But just as Biplab had imagined, it was this lion that had attracted all the attention.

For all the wrong reasons.

The scores of people outside the pandal gates, were not devotees of Ma Durga, neither the curious spectators they were hoping to attract, but activists from the Animal Rights Association, shouting out hate slogans, and waving their hand painted 'Cruelty against Animal' placards. They demanded the immediate release of all and any live animal.

If only that was all!

Within seconds of the news spreading, members of PHICH (Protection of Hinduism, Indian Culture and Heritage) arrived in truckloads with more placards. The idea of feeding raw meat to a lion, right inside Ma's home, was shocking, disgusting, and in plain Bengali unacceptable, they shouted. They formed a human chain all around Sabuj Kalyan Park, and forbade anyone to enter its premises.

All of this of course attracted even more attention. Crews from television channels and newspaper journalists photographed the picketers and interviewed the gathered crowd. News of a Pujo gone horribly wrong was flashed all over.

'How long do you think they'll be at it?' asked Bappa, slapping a mosquito that had just settled comfortably on his cheek.

'Heaven knows!' sighed Jishu. 'We've been stuck inside the club house all day. What a way to celebrate Pujo!'

'Biplab da, do something,' urged Somen. 'Are we going to stay here for the next four days? I'm starving already.'

The others murmured similar thoughts.

'It's hopeless!' sighed Biplab. 'We are doomed. And it's all my fault!' He punched his fist into the table-tennis board, sending off a cloud of dust. 'I've let you all down.'

The boys looked at each other.

'Arrey, no, no, Biplab da. No one is blaming you. It was a brilliant idea, if only the others could be made to see it,' offered Partho.

'The problem with most of these people,' added Bhombol, 'is that no one gets the subtleties. One needs to have some culture, some refinement of taste in order to be able to appreciate stuff like this. In any other country, I promise you, this would have amounted to a piece of art.'

'Let's just wait it out boys,' said Biplab Maity, his eye still on the table-tennis board. 'If any of us go out, we might be stoned. One can't really take a chance with an angry mob.'

'What I don't understand is . . . how come they chose our Pujo?' said Jishu. 'There are scores of goats being slaughtered in the name of sacrifice to the Mother Goddess, how come you don't hear of activism there?'

'It's just our luck,' whispered Biplab Maity. 'Just our rotten luck!'

He buried his face in the cup of his palms. It would take him a long time to forget this nightmare.

★

In the neighbouring *paara*, at the pandal of Milonee Club, the Mother had arrived on schedule, with her entourage. She was housed in a sky-kissing structure that represented a Japanese pagoda. The idols, thankfully not slit-eyed, were placed on a sea of floating flowers and tea-lights. The ambiance inside was that of a sanctuary, decorated with bamboo shoots and black pebbles, and with water trickling from miniature fountains. In keeping with the theme, young girls had been dressed in kimonos and their hair tied up in a bun, held in place with chopsticks. They welcomed the devotees with a bow, and guided them to the entrance of the pandal. They even performed a Japanese traditional dance at regular intervals of the day. Bollywood music had been replaced with a soft Japanese spiritual music, the kind one gets to hear in spas when one's back is getting scorched by hot stones. The area outside the pandal had been decorated like a Zen garden. A makeshift pond had been created on which floated water lilies, an arched bridge connected one side of the pond to the other. The lamp-posts had been draped with cloth-hangings on which were inscribed words of ancient Japanese wisdom, in English, Bengali and Japanese.

Several cultural programmes had been organized by the club, the most notable among them, a martial arts show by a group of Japanese men. The crowd had been enthralled by the performance, demanding to see more of it.

During the day, the air smelt of burnt camphor and sandalwood, of *dhuno* and *kashphool. Dhaakis*, their huge drums slung across their shoulders, drummed the traditional beat, the one that little children thought sounded like 'Ma Durga is here again'. Priests arrived early every morning to start the pujas, their droning chants interspersed with the banging of *kasor*, a cymbal-like instrument and *ghonta,* bells. Scores of devotees, dressed in the traditional garb, arrived in batches to offer *pushpanjali*, an offering of flowers to the goddess. The crowd was bigger than usual since devotees from the neighbouring Sabuj Kalyan club too had come here to offer their homage to the goddess. Little children struggled to keep up with the priest's chanting, the words in Sanskrit were unknown, yet familiar in a strange way. This was the language of their ancestors, the language the land had been born with. These were the holy words that spoke to the goddess, the words that carried their prayers. And no matter what one's heart desired, the goddess always listened.

★

Dashami – the last day of the Pujo. The demon Mahishasura had been killed. Evil had been thwarted. All was well with the world again.

The Sharod Samman Awards had been announced the previous day. That gave the pandal-hoppers one last day to visit the award winners, if they hadn't done that already.

This year Milonee had bagged only one award. The biggest one – the People's Choice Award for the Best-Overall Pujo. Members of Milonee Club had not forgotten to include Uday Shankar Sarani and Haripada Das Lane in their victory lap. They had paraded with the shield held high above their heads, dancing to the drumming of *dhaak,* crying out in chorus '*Milonee Club Zindabad*!',and 'Hip Hip Hooray!'.

Later, in an interview, Sudhir Bagchi, President of Milonee Club, was quoted saying that Bengalis were grateful to the Japanese for so much – right from Mitsubishi to Panasonic, and that it was high time we paid them homage. He had followed with a deep bow.

Today was the last day. All the horrors of the last four days were now a thing of the past, thought Biplab Maity. His heart though, refused to support that thought.

It was time for Ma Durga to return to her abode in the Kailash mountains again. She was being given a fitting farewell. Married ladies pressed sandesh into her unyielding lips, and smeared her face with vermilion. They did the same to each other. The idols were then hoisted on to the back of a lorry, decorated on all sides with blinking lights. Some children wept. The farewell of a loved one was always painful. Mothers tried to console them by assuring that the goddess would return again. Year after year.

Dhaakis started a beat. Ma Durga rode out of the neighbourhood, with young men and boys dancing wildly in front of her lorry to a hit Bollywood number. Bappa tugged vigorously at an invisible kite, Somen bobbed his head and wiggled his legs, Poltu shook his body like he had had an epileptic fit. Some chanted '*Durga Ma ki Jai,*' (All Glories to Mother Durga) or '*Aaschey, bochor abaar hobey,*' (Till next year!)

Young children touched the feet of elders, asking for their blessings. Men, young and old, hugged and wished each other '*Shubho Bijoya*'. Roshogollas and rajbhogs were being distributed freely.

Some distance away, in the quieter corners of the neighbourhood, Akhil Banerjee, Bibhuti Bose, Chandan Mukherjee and Debdas

Guha Roy, sat in the judge's living room. Points of the Agarwal case were being discussed over and over again, over tea and sweets.

'Joj Saheb, when exactly did you start suspecting Mr Agarwal?' asked Chandan Mukherjee.

'I always had my doubts. Somehow the man did not seem very genuine. All that story about acquiring original artefacts . . . Jahangir's wine jug, Maharaja's hookah . . . ' he shook his head. 'I thought about the evening long and hard, and it was simply impossible for someone to have taken the ring without the others noticing it. That bothered me a lot! Why did this man insist that the ring was stolen?'

'And how did you connect him to Sujit?'

'Hmm . . . well, it was clear right from the start that Sujit was the prime suspect. Once I was sure, that the ring had not left Mr Agarwal's house, I started wondering, why is Mr Agarwal trying to frame this guy? Then I remembered something he had said during the party, in Sujit's presence. It had struck me as odd at that time, not so much for what he had said, but the manner in which he had said those words. "*Only those who were with me at that time know what I have gone through.*" Those words were meant for Sujit. A warning – I know who you are.'

'What made you think of Mr Srivastav's connection?'

'That was the toughest part, and I have to admit this came to me only at the last minute. I had earlier asked Rakshit to check if there were any other cases concerning Mr Agarwal. He had told me of Mrs Agarwal's death. That it was a case of suicide, which her brother had firmly denied. I called up the Bhowanipur Police Station and spoke to the Inspector there. He furnished me with the details. Mr Agarwal's brother-in-law's name was Pankaj Srivastav, and he lived in Kanpur.

'Kanpur! That got me thinking. Didn't I see Bikash babu make an STD call to Kanpur the morning after the theft? When I asked him if Mr Agarwal's phone line was dead, he had said "Yes". But later that day, when I met Chandan babu at the market, he mentioned that he had spoken to Mr Agarwal that morning. Was Bikash lying then? Anyway, I had not paid much attention to this and had forgotten about it. But later, it made me think. I took Mr Srivastav's phone number from the Bhowanipur police station, and went to the STD booth in the daily market. The owner of the booth knows me very well, and answered my questions willingly. It seemed that Bikash Bakshi went there often, and mostly called Kanpur. I asked him if he had a record of the number called, and he showed it to me. It was Mr Srivastav's! Once I had put all the pieces together, I called Mr Srivastav myself, telling him that I had evidence regarding his sister's death. That brought him down to Calcutta by the very next flight.'

'Brilliant deducing, moshai!' exclaimed Chandan Mukherjee.

'Joj Saheb, there is one question that has been bothering me,' said Bibhuti Bose. 'If Sujit/Sibu was going to blackmail Mr Agarwal, then why did he disguise himself and put up the pretence of being a curio seller?'

'My hunch is that Sujit did not want to reveal himself to Mr Agarwal at the very onset. So he chose a pretext, an excuse, which he knew Mr Agarwal would not be able to refuse. I'm sure, had he been alone that evening with Mr Agarwal, he would surely have made his intentions clear.'

'Moshai, this is called karma,' said Debdas Guha Roy. 'You see, if Mr Agarwal had not tried to frame Sujit falsely, his past would never have been revealed. He would have died a free man.'

'*Accha*, how did the fake ring come into your possession, Joj Saheb? Did Bikash ...?'

'Yes, exactly. Once Bikash found out that I had come to know of his plans, he readily agreed to help.'

'So you see? My hunch was right all along,' said Bibhuti Bose.

'What hunch, Bibhuti babu?'

'That Mr Agarwal was a criminal!'

'Moshai, in your eyes, everyone is a criminal!' laughed Debdas Guha Roy. Bibhuti Bose choked on his glass of lime juice. He felt his face turn red, but thankfully Debdas Guha Roy did not seem to notice it.

'Joj Saheb, I must say, you were squarely wrong about one thing,' beamed Chandan Mukherjee.

'What is that?'

'Being a detective in real life does require chasing criminals down the road. Ha, Ha!'

'Here's to ABCD!' toasted Debdas Guha Roy holding up his cup of tea.

'ABCD?' asked Bibhuti Bose. 'Oh ho, you mean for Akhil, Bibhuti, Chandan and Debdas?'

'Yes. But also for the All Bengali Crime Detectives! What do you say?'

Bibhuti Bose laughed the loudest. He could not remember the last time he had laughed this hard.

It felt good.

25 Rupa
6-7-12